BORN HEARTLESS

Lock Down Publications and Ca$h
Presents
BORN HEARTLESS
A Novel by *T.J. Edwards*

Lock Down Publications
P.O. Box 870494
Mesquite, Tx 75187

First Edition September 2019
Printed in the United States of America

Lock Down Publications
Like our page on Facebook: Lock Down Publications @
www.facebook.com/lockdownpublications.ldp
Cover design and layout by: **Dynasty Cover Me**
Book interior design by: **Shawn Walker**
Edited by: **Sunny Giovanni**

Stay Connected with Us!

Text **LOCKDOWN** to 22828 to stay up-to-date with new releases, sneak peaks, contests and more…

Thank you!

Submission Guideline.

Submit the first three chapters of your completed manuscript to ldpsubmissions@gmail.com, subject line: Your book's title. The manuscript must be in a .doc file and sent as an attachment. Document should be in Times New Roman, double spaced and in size 12 font. Also, provide your synopsis and full contact information. If sending multiple submissions, they must each be in a separate email.

Have a story but no way to send it electronically? You can still submit to LDP/Ca$h Presents. Send in the first three chapters, written or typed, of your completed manuscript to:

LDP: Submissions Dept
P.O. Box 870494
Mesquite, Tx 75187

DO NOT send original manuscript. Must be a duplicate.

Provide your synopsis and a cover letter containing your full contact information.

Thanks for considering LDP and Ca$h Presents.

Chapter 1
TJ

Beads of sweat decorated my forehead and slid down the side of my face. I could feel my perspiration along the crux of my neck. The sheet stuck to my bare skin. Every few seconds I would feel a nearly pointless breeze from the oscillating fan that set on the floor of our bedroom. The back of it was so caked with dust and gunk that it provided a sparse amount of relief, but I was thankful for it. I smacked my arm as hard as I could when a mosquito landed on it; killing it before it was able to feast on me. I situated my pillow further under my head as my eyes burned a hole in the ceiling of my bedroom that was located in the Cabrini Green Housing Projects of Chicago, Illinois. It had to be more than a hundred degrees outside, and with the humidity I was sure that it pushed things well over a hundred and ten. I was so hot that I was frustrated. I was forced to share a bedroom with my two brothers—one three years older by the name of Deion, and the other one just a year and four days younger than myself, by the name of JD.

My little sister, Marie, was four years younger than me and the second to my heart after my mother, Deborah. Not only was it incredibly hot in the house, but there were so many roaches crawling around that every time I brushed out the bed and cleared it from the insects, seconds later I would be doing it all over again. Sometimes I got so frustrated that I didn't even care. Just allowed for them to crawl all over the bed, and even myself until it began to tickle or bother me too much, then I'd be right back to brushing out the bed. The process was annoying, but I was two years away from being able to move out on my own, and thus far life had dealt me a shitty hand. One that I would learn to master for the betterment of myself and my closest beloveds.

I heard the key tinkering at the lock of the front door of our apartment. Then it was opened so wide that the knob appeared to slam into the drywall. I heard my father curse aloud, then slam the door back as hard as he could.

The vibrations were felt all the way to the mattress that I slept on without a box spring. The mattress had been donated from one of the neighbors who'd gotten her children new beds. My father had brought their old ones down to us as if it had been some major accomplishment for him to do so. He dropped them on the floor in front of me and Deion with a smile on his face. "Here. Now ya'll ain't gotta sleep on that damn floor no more." He turned the bottle of Jack Daniels up, and stepped on the mattresses on his way out of the room. I'd never forget that day.

I understand feeling like shit. Not only were the beds horribly stained, but they smelled like piss. I knew why the other mother had gotten rid of them. Being afraid of this savage of a man, me and Deion exchanged glances, but wound up keeping our comments to ourselves.

My father slammed the door again, opened it, and slammed it a third time before locking it. He fumbled with the chain and dropped the two-by-four two times. This told me that he was drunk, once again. That spelled trouble for myself, my siblings, and especially my mother.

I sat up in the bed and wiped the sweat from my face. "Fuck," I said out loud. My stomach began to turn. My mother had just gotten out of the hospital from my father breaking her left arm. The whole ordeal sent me into a depressive state. It made me want to kill my old man and every nigga that ran under him. The beatings that he rendered unto my mother were always so brutal. So long lasting and heinous.

My father was 5'10" and built like a heavy weight boxer. He had shoulder-length dreads and was were forced to wear bifocal glasses because of his bad vision. He drank heavily and tooted heroin. He was a real angry man with no patience and a short fuse. Growing up, I never for one second felt that this man loved me in the least bit.

"Deborah!" I could hear him bump into the table in the living room. The table that we all ate at as a family whenever we could find enough scraps to put together to call a meal. Though, my mother was a magician. She could make a meal out of almost anything. "Deborah!" He yelled. "Bitch, I ain't gon' call you again! Get yo' punk ass in here!" He snapped.

Now I was standing up in the middle of our bedroom with my BVD underwear on. Tighty-whiteys that were too snug in all the wrong places. My heart began to pound in my chest. I began to worry about my father's intentions for calling my mother in the middle of the night.

There was a creak of the door to their bedroom. Then, a steady patter-patter of footsteps. "What's the matter, Kalvin? I'm here." Her voice was shaky and strained. Heavy with sleep and fear.

There was the sound of a chair falling to the floor. Then the table scratched across it as well. A loud boom. Next, whimpering from my mother before a loud smack, and she began to cry at the top of her lungs, before there was series of slaps, one after the next.

"Bitch! I told you when I came home, I wanted my food on the table. I wanted it waiting on me. Now where the fuck is it?" My father growled, before slapping her more than five times.

I opened our bedroom door just as my sister bumped into me and wrapped her arms around my waist. She was twelve and shaking like a leaf. I could hear her teeth chattering together. She shook her head and hugged me tighter. "TJ, he gon' stank our mother this time. He gon' kill her. I feel it in my spirit." She began to shake even harder.

This made me angry. I hated seeing my little sister in fear of the man that was supposed to be in charge of keeping us safe and sound. But instead of protecting his family, he'd found a way to damage each one of us in his own special, cruel, unique way. I turned around and hugged her. "Don't say that, Marie. Don't wish that bullshit on our mother." I kissed her forehead, then moved her out of the way. "Come on, Deion, let's go get him off of moms before it get out of hand. He already broke her arm."

Deion yawned and reached his arms over his head. "Man, fuck that. I gotta get up early for work tomorrow, and you do too. I don't feel like hearing all of that noise, so close that door." He said this and rolled over onto his stomach, pulling the holey sheet over his head.

My eyes bugged out from my face. I was in shock and could not believe that he'd totally blew off what was taking place no more than fifty feet away from our bedroom.

Two more slaps resonated in the distance. My mother yelped and began to cry louder. I could hear the ripping of clothes, then gagging.

I rushed out of the room to discover my father straddling her. He was between her thighs, ripping her gown from her body, leaving her partially nude. Then he wrapped both of his big hands around her neck, choking her with sweat dripping off of his chin. Every so often his hips would slam forward and back. Faster and faster.

My mother was 5'5", about a hundred and thirty pounds. Caramel skinned with naturally curly hair that she'd inherited from her mother's side of the family. They were Creole, Cherokee, and African American. She was an extremely beautiful woman. Reserved, soft spoken. Humble, and very respectful. God fearing and would go to the ends of the earth for her children. How she'd managed to fall in love with a psycho like my father was still a mystery to me. But she had been with him and was a part of him ever since she was thirteen years old.

At the tender age of fourteen she'd gotten pregnant with my older brother Deion, and her parents had kicked her out into the slums of Chicago where she was forced to move in with my father's mother, Gwendolyn. Once there, she found herself completely under his thumb, and had been ever since.

My mother gagged and kicked. Her face was bright red. Her eyes bugged out of her head as my father continued to choke and screw her on the floor as if she was nothing more than garbage. This infuriated me, and I knew that I had to act, even if it would be a disaster for me. He slapped her across the face again and busted her nose.

I ran over as fast as I could and tackled him off of my mother. Wound up on top of him, holding him down with all of my might. "Pops, you tripping, man! That's my mother. You can't do that shit to her like that!" I snapped, feeling the tears well up in my eyes.

He frowned, grabbed my shoulders, and humped upward, catapulting me across the room. I landed beside the run-down couch that we used to sit on and watch the floor model color television set that was against the wall of the living room. The picture was dying out of it. Sometimes it would show in color, other times it would not. We only got four channels on this television, and two of them were the PBS station. I struggled to get up before he did, but I was too late. By the time I stood up, he hit me with a series of combinations. Two to my right jaw, and an uppercut that sent me flying on top of the glass table in the living room. I could feel specks of glass poking into my skin, stinging me. I struggled to get up, but before I could, he kicked me in the chest and knocked the wind out of my body. Scooped me up and dumped me on my back. The pain was so intense that I felt like my back was broken. I winced in pain and wanted to get up but couldn't move no matter how hard I tried in that instant.

Wham! My father hollered out in pain as my mother whacked him across the back with a big, black skillet. She raised it over her head and brought it down again. This time against the back of his head, busting it. "Get the hell off of my baby. You not gon' do him like you do me. I'll die first!"

She screamed with tears running down her cheeks. She raised it over her head again.

Deion rushed her and yanked the skillet away from her. Grabbed her by the neck and flung her into the wall so hard that the corner of it busted her forehead before she fell to the floor crying. She wound up on her knees disoriented. "Don't be hitting my daddy in his head with no fucking pan, bitch! You could kill him!" He spat with his chest heaving.

"No!" Marie screamed and ran over to assist my mother. "Mama, are you okay? Are you okay, mama? Please tell me that you are."

My mother dripped blood from her mouth and tried to stand but fell back to one knee. "I'm okay, baby. I'm okay." She said. Her teeth were red with her blood.

Deion mugged her, then raised his hand and smacked her with all of his might, knocking her back to the floor where she began to sob loudly. "Stupid bitch! You gotta stay in yo' lane. Bitches ain't supposed to be coming up against niggas. You hoes need to listen!" He raised his foot, looking as if he was ready to stomp her. His face was turned into a mean scowl.

Marie rushed him with wildly swinging arms. "I hate you, Deion! I hate you! I hate yo' fucking guts!" Her punches connected with his face twice before he kneed her in the stomach, toppling her. Grabbed her by the neck and slammed her to the floor so hard that she bounced off of it before being knocked completely out. "Bitch, stay in yo' lane too. What? You think 'cause you my sister that I won't get all up in yo' muthafuckin' ass or somethin'? Fuck that. Pops said we supposed to be kicking yo' ass now so that you don't turn into a hardheaded bitch like mama. So anytime you get out of line, I'ma—"

I rushed him, hollering. Picked him up and slammed him on top of the living room table. It broke immediately. The legs flew in four different ways. Deion winced and struggled to get up. I straddled him and began to rain one punch after the next into his face. Hard ones. The blows opened him right up. And after the fifth blow, his face was wet with blood, but I kept punching. How dare this fool think he could hit my mother? That he could talk about her as such? How dare he put his hands on my little sister—a vulnerable twelve-year-old girl? I didn't know what the fuck was going through his head, but I wasn't going.

I would protect the women of my family with my life and with no hesitation. In my opinion, the men in my family were pussies. Bullies. Dudes that saw my mother and sister as nothing more than trash, and that crushed my soul. My sister and mother were nothing more than prisoners in a house full of low-life scum. "Bitch ass nigga. Who the fuck you think you is? You gon' put yo hands on my moth—" I began.

Bam, bam, bam. The blows crashed into the back of my head. Everything went black for a split second. Then I was falling off of Deion. Looking into the eyes of JD, he held a Billy club in his right hand that was sticky with my blood. I could feel it running down my neck. I fell onto my stomach, dizzy. Rose to a push up position and threw up all over the floor because my head felt like it was spinning so bad. The whole apartment seemed to be going in a circle over and over as if I was stuck in a tornado. I needed to find my mother. To protect my sister. But I felt so weak that all I could do was stagger on my knees and fall back to my chest.

Deion got up and spit his blood that I'd cause to shed into my face. Then, he stomped me in the stomach. "Bitch ass nigga! When you gon' learn that protecting these hoes ain't gon' get you nowhere." He kicked me in the back twice, causing me to holler in pain.

I straightened up, then tried to get to my feet. Deion kicked me in the face. I fell on my back, bleeding from the mouth. Still, I tried to get to my feet, but I was so dizzy that it was impossible. "Fuck you niggas. Y'all gone' have to kill me." I spat.

"This shit ain't goin' down like this." Deion laughed, grabbed my mother by her hair and flung her next to me, then did the same to my sister Marie. "Man, these hoes ain't worth all of this. Are they? They ain't good for shit but keeping the house and popping out kids. Moms ain't even finish high school. She a trick. Marie gon' be just like her. She already got a fast ass body." He snickered.

Those comments infuriated me. I wanted to get up and fuck Deion up. Wanted to whoop JD's ass too, but I felt like my ribs were cracked. I struggled to breathe. So, I laid there weak like a pussy. Unable to defend or save my mother and sister. I felt worse than an impotent nigga on his wedding night.

My father staggered over with blood running down his neck. He pulled a Thirty-Eight Special out of his waistband and cocked the hammer. Grabbed my mother by the neck and forced the barrel into her mouth. "This bitch finna go. Bitch, you gone raise yo' hand to a Boss? Do you know what I'll do to you?" He spat into her face. Deion and JD backed up with their eyes wide open.

"Pops, what you finna do, man?" Deion asked in a shaky voice.

"I'm finna kill this bitch. Hand me one of them pillows so it don't wake up these nosey ass neighbors." He ordered Deion.

I struggled to move but could not. Tears ran out of my eyes. "Pops, chill. Kill me, nigga. Leave my mother alone. Give me her bullet," I shouted. Then, pains shot all over me from my ribs. I wanted to scream but I couldn't let them bitch ass niggas know that they had me in a sticky situation. I had to be a man for my mother. Had to get my old man to kill me instead of her.

He turned to me and lowered his eyes. "Aw, lil' nigga, don't worry, 'cause after I smoke this bitch, you're next." He promised, then put the gun back into her mouth. She whimpered around it.

"Pops, I don't think you should smoke her, man. Give the bitch one more chance. She ain't mean to not have your dinner ready. It just ain't nothing to eat in the house. We ate peanut butter on a spoon, and syrup sandwiches. I swear." Deion assured him.

My father lowered his head and shook it. "So, you trying to call me a failure, too. You trying to say this my fault?" He asked, mugging Deion. Then, he pointed the gun at him.

Deion broke out of the room. Rushed into our bedroom and slammed the door. He knew my pops was nuts. He wasn't taking no chances on being shot, and I couldn't blame him.

JD slowly eased out of the room and into the bathroom where he closed the door. My father put the barrel on my mother lips and twisted it sideways. "Bitch, I should kill you. I should knock yo' fucking head off of your shoulders. Got blood running all down my neck and shit." He spat on the floor then looked over to Marie who was still knocked out. The way she was lying on the floor, her nightgown was up around her stomach, exposing her white panties that had hearts all over them. My father smiled and stood up. Grabbed a handful of my mother's hair, bringing her to her feet, then slammed her against the wall. "If you ever put yo' hands on me again, or if I ever come home and ain't no food on that table, bitch, I'm killing you. You ain't got no more chances with me. You got that?" He asked this question with his forehead against hers.

She nodded with tears running down her cheeks. "Yes, baby, I understand you. It will never happen again. I promise."

He smiled and looked down at Marie. "Good. Now take my daughter in there and get her clean. Since me and you ain't seeing eye to eye right now, you sleep in there with the boys, and my baby gon' sleep with me. I need to apologize for what took place tonight. I ain't mean for her to get hurt like she did." He threw my mother to the floor beside Marie.

"JD, get yo punk ass out of the bathroom so they can wash up." I used the wall to make it to my feet.

My father walked over to me and placed the barrel of his gun against my neck. "TJ, if you ever try and get in the way of how I handle me and mines again, I'ma send you to the Reaper; you dig me?"

I stared at him for a long time before I nodded. I hated this man and had ever since I was old enough to understand that he really wasn't a man at all. But a coward. What type of man did the things he did to his family? What type of man had his family living in a run-down ass Project building with rats the size of cats, and roaches that were the size of new-born birds?

How could he beat my mother for not providing his dinner when he wasn't man enough to provide her the meal that would need to be cooked? He forbade her to work, or to leave the house, period. He was verbally, physically, and most assuredly emotionally abusive. He wanted everything his way, yet he refused to provide the necessary tools for a person to meet him even half way. My father was a joke. A clown. A pussy to me. A low life. A boy fronting to be a man. One that ruled our family with fear and torment. I had to get my mother and sister from under his rule. I had to get us out of the projects. I didn't care if I died making it happen for the ladies of my family; I would be their sacrifice. And I would die for them happily. So, as I nodded, a million thoughts were running through my mind. All pertaining to the safety and well-being of my mother and sister. I had to find a way to make it happen. Had to rise above the gutters of the Cabrini Green Projects. Had to rescue my peoples.

Chapter 2

My Pops was one of them lazy type of niggas. On top of that, he was real selfish, and the kind of man that liked to lay back and have shit handed to him instead of him going out and working for it himself. Our rent was $400 every single month, and even though I was only sixteen at this time, I was responsible for paying it. Because I was, and hadn't stepped off into the game yet, I was forced to get a punk ass job working as a cook for a place called Harold's Chicken. One of the sistas from the Projects that went to our church ran into a hefty settlement from the government because she had gotten hit by a bus while crossing the street of Cottage Grove. The bus left her in a wheelchair for six months, and by the time she jumped out of it she was awarded $3-million and used some of that cash to cop her a few restaurants. I worked in the one that she had on the northwest side of Chicago. It was a nice lil' joint. Clean, and the best part about it was that a lot of females from my high school worked there as well.

Eight out of the ten that worked there were bad. But to me there was none badder than this lil' caramel chick named Punkin. She was about 5'5" with dark brown eyes, a slight gap in her upper row of teeth, and even though she had to rock a uniform, she always found a way to make it look good on her. Whether she was rocking a pair of fresh Jordan's with it, or had her hair done in such a way, or made sure that her few pieces of jewelry offset her pretty features just right, she made that uniform look good. She was also strapped like a muthafucka and had been ever since we were in seventh grade. She had these long eyelashes that looked fake but were authentic. She was slightly bow-legged too. I found that sexy. She was originally from Gary, Indiana but had moved to Chicago in the seventh grade after her old man got gunned down by some Gangster Disciples out that way. He'd been killed right in front of her. The gunmen had turned the gun on her to smoke her as well, but when it came time for him to pull the trigger, the gun jammed, so he took off running. The story was a bit tragic to me, and after getting to know Punkin I was thankful that his gun had jammed. Punkin was a real quiet and reserved female, but always found a way to stand out without even trying. And she always smelled good. For me, a female's scent was very important.

Even though Harold's was a place of work, for the employees it was also somewhat of a tennis shoe fashion show. You were able to show your individuality by the shoes you rocked. Because my family was dirt poor, and all of my money went toward the bills, I was unable to be up to par. I found myself rocking a pair of worn down British Knights. They were all white with the gum-bottom. I kept them in the best condition that I possibly could by using the white shoe polish from the corner store. I painted them every three days, and every time I had to, I felt like shit.

I hated being poor. I felt like the whole world had money except for me and my family. I felt on many days that God had forgotten about us.

A month before my seventh birthday I walked into the restaurant to find Punkin behind the register serving a customer. The place was empty with the exception for the older sister she was serving, and the other workers had yet to get there. When I opened the door, she glanced in my direction. The sunlight reflected off of her Sephora lip gloss. Her lips were popping and already naturally juicy. But this day they looked real good to me. I couldn't help staring at 'em.

She smiled and gave me a nod as I walked behind the counter past her, heading to the employee unisex dressing room. "What's good, TJ? I see you're here early. What gives?"

"My uncle gave me a ride, so I ain't have to wait on the bus," I said and kept it moving. I always felt some type of way around her because she was so well put together. Every time I saw Punkin she was always fresh and smelled so, so good.

"That's what's up. I'll be back there to holler at you in a minute. Let me finish ringing her up."

The lady in front of her crossed her arms over her chest and exhaled loudly. She was a big girl, so I imagined that she was ready to chow down on some Harold's Chicken. I couldn't blame her for that. Because I worked in the restaurant, and often closed, the chicken was what me and the family feasted on most nights. It was another way I helped to provide for the family.

Before I could step into the small dressing room in the back, the owner, Jackie, came out of her office and blocked my path. She had a smile on her face when she looked over my shoulder into the front of the restaurant where Punkin was working on a customer and gave me the come here signal with her index finger. I dropped my bag on the bench inside the dressing room and kicked it closer to my locker. I'd brought it because I needed to steal a few rolls of tissue and liquid soap. We'd run out of shampoo and bars of soap at home. So, I had to fill in those blanks. I was also supposed to steal as much chicken as I could. Some that was already cooked and some frozen ones. So, I kept that in mind as I followed her into her office.

She was standing at the door. After waiting for me to walk in, she closed it behind me. I took a seat in the lone chair in front of her desk. Jackie was about 5'2", dark skinned with a prominent mole right under her right eye. She had to be every bit of my mother's age. She had a real nice body, and always bragged about running track back in high school. I could tell that she had been athletic because her body was right.

She had these real big titties that were always on display. Most times I tried to avoid looking at them because I had a lot of respect for her and she was the Deacon's wife at our church. Deacon Blakemore was a pillar in our community.

He hosted cookouts, block parties, gave away free turkeys at Thanksgiving, and was running to be an Alderman for our ward. He was a good dude from as far as I could see.

Jackie stepped away from the door, came in front of where I was sitting and took a seat on her desk after moving her laptop out of the way. She pulled her tight skirt back and crossed her thick thighs. Licked her juicy lips that were painted red. "How is your mother doing, TJ? Your daddy ain't been messin' her up, has he?" She flipped her weave over her shoulder.

I didn't even know how to answer this question because it was too personal, if you asked my honest opinion. So, I just looked up at her and didn't say nothing.

She smiled weakly as she pulled the hem of her skirt up a little more so that I could see the tops of her stockings. They were black and appeared to be hooked to something underneath her skirt. I felt my piece stir in my Girbaud jeans. "I know it ain't my business, so maybe I shouldn't have asked that question, but I do worry about her from time to time. I wish I could help her some more, but giving you a job here has to be a start, right?" She spread her thighs just a bit. Now I could smell her perfume mixed with the heat and scent of her basement parts. It had me feeling some type of way to say the least.

I nodded and did all that I could to not look directly between her thighs. And since I was trying not to it's like she opened them a little further. Far enough for me to see her crotch band mold the lips of her kitten. I could even see the space in between each gap where the thighs met her groin. "We definitely appreciate you for this gig. I know I ain't got my worker's permit yet, but my school counselor is supposed to be drawing it up for me and signing off for me to work over six hours. Hopefully I'll have it by tomorrow." I wondered if that was the reason she called me into her office. I felt real weird being in there with her, especially with the door being closed. I also wanted to steal a few minutes of conversation with Punkin before the other kids got there. They would surely be all up in her face. I loved chopping it up with her.

She waved me off. "You know I ain't worried about that, TJ. Whether you get it or not, I'ma let you work here. I gotta keep some good looking young men in my establishment. You remind me of my high school boyfriend. He had plenty muscles just like you. And some deep ass dimples. I wish I could adopt you." She snickered and opened her legs wider. "Do you know why I called you in here?" She looked into my eyes and grabbed her laptop.

I shook my head and glanced up at the digital clock on her office wall. I should have started work ten minutes ago. I was sure that my window for hollering at Punkin had passed. That got me annoyed. "N'all, what's good?"

She turned the laptop around, staring at me. Hit the key and handed it to me. "That's you on there, stealing food out of the coolers, and putting them into your gym bag. I expected more from you. Care to explain?" She rubbed her inner thigh.

I looked at the screen and saw myself looking both ways before I opened the chicken cooler and rushed inside of it with my bag. Once inside, I was filling it up like a true crook. I was embarrassed. There was no way that I could deny it being me. The footage was so clear that I could make out the deep wave pattern on top of my head. "Yo, Miss Jackie, I'm sorry. It's just real messed up at the crib right now. Our fridge is leaking. I mean that both literally and figuratively. I just wanted to make sure that I put some food on the table for the family. Please don't fire me. I'm in charge of the rent and some of the utilities." Man, I felt like crap. I wished that I hadn't had to stoop to such antics, but it was the life I lived. Ever since I'd been alive all I knew was the struggle. My family never had anything other than rats and roaches. It was crazy.

She took the laptop back and set it beside her. "Boy, I ain't gon' fire you. You forget that I'm from the Projects too. I know how it is. I just wish you would have talked to me. That way I could have helped you out, instead of us being in this awkward position." She sucked on her bottom lip. "But I think I know how to rectify this situation." She rubbed along her thick, chocolate thighs and opened them wider. Her fingers danced over the crotch band. "Come and smell me here." She pressed the panties into her lips and moaned deep within the back of her throat. "Come on, baby."

I slowly got out of the chair, nervously, feeling like this was a set up. My piece jumped in my pants. "You for real, Miss Jackie?" I asked looking between her legs.

She nodded. "Yeah, baby, bring yo lil' young self over here and smell me. I need you to get a whiff of my scent. I got plans for your lil' fine ass." She reached for my head.

I stepped close enough to her so she could place her hand on top of my head. Once there, she guided it downward until my face was in between her thick legs. I placed my nose on her crotch and sniffed.

This made her shudder. "Again, baby. Sniff me again." I did this a second time. Once again she shuddered, but yanked her panties to the side, exposing one of the meatiest pussies I had ever seen in my life, even to this day. She peeled open the lips. Her inner pink was glistening with her fluids. "Kiss me right on this lil' nipple right here." She licked her pointer finger and rubbed it in a circular motion around her clitoris.

Being this close I could smell a nice hint of her vagina. It smelled like perfume and a copper penny. The scent aroused me right away. I leaned as close as I needed to, took my lips and kissed her grown pussy. Right on the clitoris.

She bucked forward and forced me further between her legs by pressing on the back of my head. I could feel her acrylic nails on the top of my neck, digging into my skin. "Uh! Now lick it up and down, TJ. You acting like you never did this before, baby." Her thighs opened further. She took two fingers and spread her sex lips as far apart as she could. There was a clear line of juice oozing out of her box. It slid out of her hole onto the crack of her dark brown ass cheeks, making her crack shine.

I raised my head. "I haven't." I didn't know why I admitted that to her, but I guess a part of me wanted her to know because I didn't want her to look at me from then on out as if I was slow or something. I mean, I was sixteen so I guess I should have eaten my share of cat by then, but being that my family was so poor, I was always working a dead end job at one place or another. I didn't fit in at school because everybody there stayed fitted in the best gear, and my clothes were always outdated and mediocre at best. Wasn't no females trying to creep with me like that. At least I didn't think so.

She closed her thighs around my face and started to hump up from her desk. "It's okay, baby, I'ma train you then. I'ma show you everything that you need to know. It's gon' be our little secret," she said through a strained voice, stopping on occasion to catch her breath. She rotated her hips in a big circle, riding my face, moaning under her breath with her head thrown back.

Her breasts were threatening to spill over the top of her bra the last time I'd looked up at her. My face was dripping wet with her juices. Her scent was so heavy at this point that I could barely breathe. Her thighs had me trapped. Besides that, my dick was so hard because I couldn't believe that Miss Jackie was letting me kiss in between her crack like I was. She was the first grown woman to take an interest in me. It was exciting. I kept getting images in my head of her being at church, acting all holier than thou and shit. That made it ten times hotter to me. I felt her cream running down my neck and into my shirt.

"I'm cumming, baby. I'm cumming. Uh, lil' boy, you making me cum." She ground my face into her particulars and came hard.

I kept my tongue out, licking up and down her crease off instinct. Sucking on the lips like I saw the females do in the porno movies. This drove her crazy, because right after the first one, she came again, and pushed me away from her.

"Let me see yo thang, TJ. Hurry up because you gotta get to work."

She slid her hand into her center and played with the lips, smushing them together, creating a thick gel of juice. She'd take that gel and rub it around her clitoris. I wiped my mouth and got a lil' nervous. This was a grown woman asking to see my piece. I didn't know if it was big enough to show off as of yet, or if it wasn't. I'd never had a chance to mess around with any female, so I didn't know what to judge it in comparison to. I had seen my older brother Deion's and I knew that mine was fatter and longer than his, but he was only three years older than me. Miss Jackie had to be in her late thirties or early forties. I figured that the men she messed around with had to have had forty years to grow their pieces, so they had to be way bigger than me.

She licked her lips and slid a finger into herself. "Come on, baby. Just let me see how it look. I'm curious." She hopped off the desk and squatted before me, rubbing her hand over the front of my jeans. "It feel real big." She licked the denim and began to unbutton me. Once she had my jeans open, she pulled them down far enough for my dick to spring up, poking against my drawers. She yanked them down, exposing my shaft. The head was the shade of purple. The long body was thick with veins all over it. She moaned in the back of her throat and wrapped her hand around the body. Leaned forward and licked all around the head before sucking it into her mouth. She looked up at me with her jaws hollowed out. It felt so hot in there that my toes began to curl. She was twirling her tongue around the helmet over and over. Teasing my pee hole. Then she would suck up and down it in a fast pace. Her bobbing made her breasts pop out of her top. Both were displayed. The nipples were puffy and erect. One sight of them and it was too much for me. This was a grown woman touching my pipe. A woman from our church. Sucking me like she was. It was too much. When she ran her hand up my left thigh and cupped my balls, I came hard, jerked and humping into her mouth. She continued to suck and swallow me, moaning around my knob until she had her feel and I was running away from her because my piece had become real sensitive.

She got up and wiped her mouth, fixing her bra and licking her juicy lips. "Damn, I wish I could adopt your ass. If you was my lil' boy, I'd teach you everything you need to know about a woman's body, and I wouldn't care who knew about it because you would belong to me. All I got is daughters, so I'll never be able to teach my Lil' man something." She shook her head and stepped closer to me, grabbing my still very hard dick, squeezing it in her hand. "I wasn't expecting you to have all this meat either." She kissed my lips. "I got a proposition for you. You say your family is in need of food and stuff right?" She was stroking my pipe and it was feeling so good.

I closed my eyes. "Yeah, it's real rough right now. Damn, Miss Jackie."

She licked my neck. "Well, I'ma help you load up y'alls cabinets and refrigerator three times a month, but in exchange I wanna be your teacher. I want you to let me play Mommy. How does that sound?" She took me by the dick and rubbed the head up and down her wet slit. I could feel her folds sliding all over me.

It felt so good. Even though her request was super weird to me, I saw the benefits in her proposal right away. If I could fill up our house with food three times a month that would take a lot of the burden off of my mother. She'd be able to have my pops' meals ready for him whenever he chose to slide into the house. That would prevent her from receiving a lot of beatings and I didn't know how many more of them

I could witness without me flat out taking his life. So, anything that I could do to help our family I was down to do it. I waited for her to pick her face up from the crux of my neck, looked into her eyes and nodded with my piece poking her sex lips. The helmet was wedged in between her gap. I was hoping she was about to let me sample that pussy right then and there. I was more than ready to discover that part of a woman's anatomy.

She kissed my lips. "Okay then." She humped forward so that my dick slid in just enough to feel her heat, then moved backward and pulled her skirt down. I was devastated. She opened the top drawer to her desk and handed me a cell phone. "Here. When I get things situated with my husband I'ma call you so we can begin our lessons. In the meantime, take this." She handed me a Link, or Food Stamp card. "This card has five hundred dollars left on it. Do whatever you need to for your family, baby, but just remember that nothing is free in this world. Everything costs. It's cool that you wanna do for your family, but it comes at a price. You're closing tonight and you can have whatever we don't sellout of that is already cooked. Don't let me catch you stealing from me again or there will be consequences. You feel me?" She waited until I nodded before she sat in her leather seat and crossed her thick thighs. "Alright then, we understand each other. Now gon' get to work. Mama will see you soon. Keep your mouth shut."

I left her office feeling both excited and like a lame. Excited because I knew I was going to be hitting some grown pussy, and that I was going to be able to place that food stamp card into my mother's hands so she could hit up Aldi's and do her thing. But I also felt like a lame because of how she was talking to me like I wasn't shit. And to be honest, at this time, I wasn't.

Chapter 3

It felt real good to watch my mother load up two grocery carts full of food. While Marie pushed one, she pushed the other, humming to herself. Every so often she'd stop, just so she could hug me and kiss me on the cheek. "Baby, you don't know how proud I am of you. I don't know how you obtained this card, but it ain't my business to know. All I care about is the fact that you're safe, and that we will be okay for a while. I get our stamps next week, and I'll add what we got on that card with this one. We should more than make it. Uh, I love you so much, TJ. I don't know why you do what you do, or how you are like you are, but I thank Jehovah for you. You're my very own blessing." She kissed my cheek again, leaving behind a red lipstick imprint.

Whenever my mother said things like this, or kissed my cheek, it always made me feel so good. I loved to see her smile. Loved to know that she'd have one less worry if I could figure something out. She was my heart and soul. My purpose in life. I knew that I was going to move her out of the Projects. Knew that I was going to find a way to buy her house and to get her from under my father's abusive thumb. She was a queen and needed to be treated as such.

I wrapped my arm around her shoulder and kissed her soft cheek. "I got you, mama. For as long as I am alive, I got you. You too, lil' sis." I said this looking down at Marie.

She smiled up at me and rolled her eyes, blushing. She was so beautiful. A spitting image of my mother.

Deion came from one of the aisles in Aldi's with four boxes of cereal. He dropped them into Marie's cart and bumped her out of the way. "All of dem Captain Crunch are mine. If I catch anybody eating my cereal, I'ma tear they head off. I mean that shit. Straight up." He looked from Marie to my mother, then to me.

I was frowning, heated. Not only had he bumped my sister out of the way recklessly, but his mouth in front of my mother was too disrespectful for my taste. I couldn't understand why he didn't view her like the queen she was. Instead, it was like my brother looked at her as if she was nothing more than human trash. That irritated me. Made me want to do something real foul to his ass.

"Nigga, what you looking all crazy for?" He asked, stepping past my mother to stand inches from me.

"Deion, you need to watch yo' mouth in front of our mother. Don't you see her standing right here, bruh? Dang." I felt my blood pressure rising and tried to calm down by breathing through my mouth. I knew my temper was bad, and whenever Deion was around it was even worse. He ain't have no respect for nobody.

He shrugged. "So what? She done heard me curse before. Shit, she do it, too. I'm grown," he said looking me up and down. Then he looked over to my mother who was looking off as if she couldn't hear what was being said. "Why you got a problem with my mouth, mama?"

She shrugged. "Baby, don't worry. When we get home, we'll put your name on your cereal so nobody will mess with them. Your best bet is to keep them away from your father."

"That's why I got 'em. He don't like Captain Crunch. He say they're too sweet. So, I ain't gotta worry about him. But I said what I said. No more warnings. When I get home, I'ma tell JD what it is because his chubby ass be trying to eat up every thang; even the rats in the crib." He laughed at his own joke, then grew serious. "But y'all make sure y'all don't touch 'em."

Marie placed her hand on her hip and frowned. "Boy, you ain't paying for nothing in these carts. How is it that you're the oldest and you don't help out at all? Only man we really got in the house is TJ. That's ridiculous." She rolled her eyes and popped her neck. Her long hair fell down her back in loose curls. One of my mother's friends from church had taken her shopping, and on this day she'd chosen to wear the Prada skirt dress; purple and black. It made her look older than her twelve years. She rocked a pair of Steve Madden's, open toed. She'd painted every other toe purple, or black. Like myself, my sister did whatever she had to, to stay fitted. She didn't let our poor circumstances bind her.

Deion scoffed. "Bitch, you don't buy shit either. You're just like me. You're a fucking bum. Don't get shit twisted. I'll slap the fuck out of you in this store, in front of all these people. You know how I get down." He said and took a step in her direction. She left her cart and ran behind me. Deion stepped into my face, with his nostrils flared. Looked me in the eye and sucked his teeth. "Fuck she running behind you for like you gon' do somethin'? They think you the shit just because you be saving these hoes. Nigga, I'll prove to them that you ain't on nothin'. On everything." He stepped all the way into my face until our noses were touching.

My blood was boiling. I was so heated that my vision was going blurry. My heartbeat rapid in my chest. "Bruh, you good. When we get home, just put the cereal up. Neither of us will touch it. Aiight." I said this looking into his eyes. I didn't fear this nigga, and I knew for a fact I could whoop him because I had before. But I had to take the high road. I wanted my mother to enjoy the relief that the groceries would provide. I didn't want her to be stressing or having to deal with a house full of arguing and fighting for one night. I knew that if I fed into Deion's bullshit that it would only escalate to me putting hands on him. I ain't have no problem with that, but like I said I had to keep my mother at the forefront of my mental at all times. She was special to me. So, I was forced to give up small battles with Deion to win the long-term war.

He nodded. "Yeah, nigga, just like I thought. Stay in yo' lane." He bumped me and walked toward a group of four females that were just coming into the store.

I made eye contact with Punkin right away. I felt a weird feeling go through me.

"I swear to God I hate Deion. Why didn't you just whoop him, TJ? He know he can't mess with yo' business. Even mama know that; don't you, mama?" Marie said, looking up toward our mother who was picking through spices.

I slid behind her and kissed her neck on the side. "Ma, don't answer that. It's good." I hugged her tight. "Just keep gettin' ya carts ready, and when you're done checking out, I'll help you carry them to the car. A Lil' chick just walked in, and I wanna go over and say what's good to her, okay?"

She nodded. "Gon' head, baby. I should be done in about thirty minutes or so." She looked around until she laid eyes on the group of girls and smiled. "Which one you feeling?" She asked.

"The Lil' caramel one in that Tommy dress. I got this weird thing for her." I had to admit it out loud to somebody.

Marie smacked her lips. "You just like her because she got that big ol' booty. You ain't slick." She snickered.

My mother popped her. "Girl, shut up. Gon' head, baby. We'll see you in a minute." I walked off.

"TJ, our Lil' apartment ain't big enough for no baby mamas!" Marie hollered. "That girl ready to be impregnated."

I couldn't help laughing at her crazy ass. My sister was super funny to me. Funny and real. I could tell that when she grew up she was going to be a force to be reckoned with.

When I made it over to Punkin she was talking on her cell phone with a smile on her pretty face. I could tell that her eyebrows were recently arched. Her nails were done, and her hair looked fresh as well. She smelled real good, and her dress was hugging her just right. Her curves were on display in a tasteful manner. I even peeped her toes. They were fresh as well. I knew that she was way out of my league. But there was just something that drew me to her.

When she saw me get closer she ended her call and smiled up at me. "What's good, TJ? I see you out shopping with your mother and stuff. That's what's up." Her lips were super shiny. Juicy. They looked good. I wondered how they tasted.

"Aw, yeah, Chicago real crazy. I just wanna make sure that she can do her shopping without nothing happening to her. That's my heart right there." I looked over my shoulder to see my mother explaining one of the seasonings to my sister. Marie nodded and paid close attention. "What brings you out?"

"Aw, I'm having my Sweet Sixteen birthday party this Friday. I gotta get a bunch of snacks for the low. Aldi's is the place to do all of that, so here I am. Well, me and my lil' crew." She nodded at the other three girls that my brother were flirting with.

They were all up in his grill. Deion was a real pretty boy, so I understood. Plus, he was into boosting clothes, so he was always fitted from head to toe in the latest of fashions. I envied that but knew my time would come soon.

"Damn, you only fifteen?" I was shocked. Punkin was built like a grown ass woman and carried herself as such. I would have never guessed that she was younger than me. She too fine.

She blushed. "Yeah, dang. How old you thought I was? We are in the same grade." She rolled her eyes.

"Yeah, I keep forgetting that part. But anyway, why I ain't got no invitation yet? What? 'Cause my gear ain't up to par I ain't worthy to celebrate your day or something?" I said it in a joking manner, but a part of my feelings were hurt. I really liked her and needed to find an in to be able to get at her.

She sucked her teeth. "Boy, I don't care about all that. I didn't even think you'd want to come. But if you really do, you're more than welcome. Here." She opened her Tommy purse and handed me an invitation, just as her Puerto Rican friend with the light brown eyes came over.

Her name was Sodi and she was just as fine as Punkin. She had long, curly hair that fell to her waist. Was slim, with a nice booty, and her gear stayed on point. She was one grade below us.

I took the invitation and read it over. "This what's up. Do you want me to bring you anything in particular?" I asked hoping she didn't because I ain't have no scratch no way.

She shook her head. "N'all, just come and celebrate me. I'm cool with that." She stepped forward and gave me a short hug.

Sodi cleared her throat and stepped into my face, holding her hand up to me. "Hey, Papi, your name is Thylonius, right?"

I laughed at hearing her pronounce my name with a heavy Spanish accent. It sounded sexy to me. "Yeah, but everybody call me TJ, so you can too." I held my arms open for her.

She ain't waste no time stepping into them or hugging me close. She kissed my neck and stood back. I was shocked because she was so damn bad. "You work with Punkin, right? Over at the Harold's place?"

I nodded.

"Well, look, I'm from the westside, and I don't know how y'all do it over here on the northwest, but where I come from, we go for what we know. I think you're fine as fuck, and I wanna get up with you. I love a nigga with all them muscles that you got. I'm little, and I need to be protected. What's good?"

Punkin scoffed and crossed her arms in front of her. "Damn, Sodi, you didn't see us talking? You're being rude."

Sodi shook her head. "No, I'm not. Besides, I waited until you guys were done, and you already got a man. I need one too, and it gotta be somebody like his fine ass." She turned to me. "TJ, what's good?" Her light brown eyes were popping hard. Then I peeped her long ass hair that looked shiny. She was fitted in a Prada dress that hugged her lil' curves too. She ain't really have no breasts like that, but the little bit she did have fit her frame just right. I was feeling

32

her to say the least. I was also thrown for a loop at hearing that Punkin already had a man. That kind of irritated me.

Punkin stood there for a second, then exhaled loudly. "Well, anyway, I'ma step away so y'all can holler. I'll see you at the party, TJ." She walked away looking defeated.

I wanted to chase her and find out what was good with this other nigga that Sodi was speaking on, but Sodi blocked my path and smiled up to me. Damn, it sucked that she was so bad. We wound up exchanging numbers and she became my girl officially two days later. That same day, Miss Jackie hit me up and told me to meet her at her house over in Evanston. So, after helping my mother put away the groceries, I jumped on the Brown-line EL train, took that over to the Red-line, and rode it out to Evanston. When I got off the train and went to the bottom of the staircase, Miss Jackie was waiting in her Benz along the curb. She tapped her horn twice just as the sun lowered itself behind the clouds. I jumped in, and she grabbed me by the shirt and pulled me over to her.

"Mama want you so bad, baby. I can't wait until we get home."

She took my hand and slid it under her short skirt. My fingers landed on her soft pussy lips. I played in between her crack, searching for her hole. When I found it, I slid my middle finger all the way inside of her. Her pussy was hot and ready.

"Uh, yeah, baby. You feel how hot I am? Wait until you get that lil' young dick inside of me. It's gon' feel so good. Trust me. Now taste that finger." She ordered, throwing her whip into drive and pulling away from the curb.

I sucked my finger into my mouth and tasted her salty flavor. For some reason it aroused me. She had been my first taste of pussy, and for me it was glorious.

We pulled up to her home about ten minutes later. Before I could make it through her door good enough she was ripping my shirt from my body, and kicking the door closed.

She licked all over my exposed chest, down to my stomach muscles. Biting on the abs and licking in between the deep valley that separated the muscles on each side. The whole time her tongue went to work, her hands were taking my pants off of me. My dick sprung out like a brown cucumber with a purple head attached to it.

She stroked it and fell to her knees, sucked me into her mouth and speared her head into my crotch over and over again, taking me as deep as possible. Gagging, and still going like a pro. My lil' young ass was whimpering and everything. Her head game had me perplexed. I could barely breathe, and my toes were curled up in my shoes. Sweat appeared along my forehead and her place was well air conditioned.

"Miss Jackie. Miss Jackie. I'm about to cum already. I'm about to cum." This made her suck me harder and faster. Her gagging intensified. She added more spit and concentrated on the top of my head. Nipping it with her teeth. Pulling and tugging. It became too much for me to handle.

I came hard. She held my dick away from her mouth and allowed me to squirt into it from a short distance. I watched my cum spit into her mouth. She swallowed it, then sucked me back into her lips. Moaning loudly. Her hand went between her legs, fingering her pussy. I could tell because her arm was going back and forth.

After she got me back hard within seconds, she stood up and grabbed my hand. "Come on, son. I want you to fuck me while I bend over the kitchen table. I'm so tired of cooking this man's meals. At least now I'll know that every time I gotta put a plate in front of his ass that you'd fucked me right on that table in there." She sucked her bottom lip and pulled me along. Once inside of there she hiked up her skirt and bent over the table. Once again she was rocking a pair of garters that were attached to her stockings. She looked so sexy and was slowly making me fall in love with lingerie. I felt it made a female look so alluring. I knelt and sniffed her pussy from the back. Planted my nose right on her hole and inhaled as hard as I could.

She arched her back and moaned. "Yeah, son, sniff me, baby. Then take out that young meat and fuck me the right way. The way he ain't done in years." She spread her thighs, giving me access.

I stood up, stroking my piece. Pulling the skin all the way back before lowering the head to her sex lips.

As soon as I touched her there with it she shivered. Her knees threatened to buckle. I worked the head just past her pussy lips. Watched the brown folds open to reveal her inner pink. Then my pole was sliding inside of her. It got hotter and hotter. Her slit was tight, unbelievably. I slid all the way in and rested with my hips against her thick ass cheeks. They were pushed inward because of the weight I laid upon them.

She reached under herself and felt our connection. "Uh. Son, now fuck me hard. Please. Fuck this grown pussy. Fuck me and I'll look out for you." She lowered her straps, and her titties came spilling out of her top. They were juicy with Hershey Kiss-like nipples attached to them. She rocked forward and then backward, allowing me to run in and out of her. "Grab my hips. Use them to help you and do it hard. Punish me. Please."

I did exactly what she ordered. Grabbed her hips, pulled back as far as I could go, then slammed forward. She felt so soft and mushy inside. Her heat felt like it was scorching me.

I got so excited seeing all of that ass that I started to rock back and forth with my knees bent just enough to give me the perfect angle. My speeds increased. Every time I crashed into her, her ass would jiggle along with her breast. It all looked so fucking good to me. I wished that I could stay there fucking her forever.

"Uh. Uh. TJ. Son. Aw, baby. Fuck me. Fuck me. Oh, yes. Faster. Harder. Um!" She slammed back into my lap, impaling herself on my shaft. Her breasts rocked on top of the table. She stretched her arms all the way out and laid her face on top of the table, knocking a few placemats to the floor. "Yes, son. Fuck mama. Fuck me harder. Shit, yes."

I couldn't believe that a church woman could use such language, but it was turning me on like crazy. The more she talked, the harder I hit that pussy, until I got the hang of it. I began hitting that shit so hard that she was begging me to slow down. But that motivated me to speed up the pace. She came, screaming at the top of her lungs, buckled and fell to the floor with me on top of her, still fucking away, plunging deeper and deeper. Her juices were pouring out of her, dripping off of my sex parts. I was close to cumming. I forced her leg to her side, cuffed it, killing that pussy as hard as I could.

"TJ, TJ, you're killing me, son. Uh, fuck, you're killing this pussy. I'm cumming! I'm cumming, son!" She started to shake.

Her walls sucked at me, and as soon as they did I came while biting on the back of her neck, growling. It was the first time I came inside of a woman, and it felt so good. Miss Jackie was the reason I started to desire older women. After our session, we showered and climbed into her bed.

She climbed on top of me and laid her face in the crux of my neck. "That was amazing, baby. You know just how to do mama, don't you?" She kissed my neck and opened her thighs wider. I could feel her pussy searing my stomach.

Every time she referred to herself as my mother it threw me for a loop. It made my real mother flash into my mind, and that creeped me out. It would always take me a few seconds to get her image out of my head. But after a while I got used to her forbidden titles and rolled with the punches.

She kissed my lips and licked them. "I wanna take you shopping, son. Gotta make sure you stay looking good for me. I can't have you out there looking all Barna and shit, you know what I mean?" She kissed me again on the lips.

Now my hands roamed around until I was cuffing her ass. It felt soft. She moaned into my neck. "I was finna say.

ain't no sense of me having a bad older woman if you ain't gon' keep me fresh, mama. You can't have your son out here looking all ratchet," I said, playing into her fantasy of mother and son.

She shivered, licked along my neck humped into me, and moaned. "Oh, so now that you got some of Mama, you gon' hit my pockets, huh?" She giggled and looked into my eyes; sucking on her bottom lip all sexy like. Her dark skin was appealing to me. That and those juicy ass lips. I even liked the few moles that decorated her naked breast. She also had a few stretch marks that looked good to me, too. I think I was becoming older woman crazy because of her, and I was cool with that.

"I just wanna be up to par, and I know you're holding your own. I know you got me. You're my moms, right?" I slid my fingers into her crease from the back. My hard dick was already at full mass. I picked her up and slid her down on it. "Right, mama?"

She closed her eyes and nodded. "Right. Un. I got you, baby. I got you, I swear." She placed both her palms on my chest and began to ride me slowly, taking all of my dick. Moaning with her head thrown backward. Her soft, pretty breasts were jiggling on her chest. She looked like an African goddess.

I didn't know why she was so screwed up mentally when it came to forbidden sex, but her pussy was good to me. Real good. I knew that I wanted to dive in and out of it a lot. I let her ride me until she came two more times then fell on top of me. Before I left at two in the morning she handed me her Master Card and told me that I had a limit of $3,000 to get me a few clothing items. I felt like a boss by the time I jumped back on the El train riding back home to the Projects.

Chapter 4

Even though I didn't fuck with niggas like that, I had this one homie from the Projects that I'd grown up with. His name was Juelz, and we started out as enemies. When we were little, around five and six, every time we saw each other all we did was fight for no reason at all. I just didn't like him. It was probably because everybody said that we looked like twins, and I didn't appreciate that one bit. I was my own person and hated to be linked in with another nigga. I've always been that way, but around the age of eleven me and Juelz got real cool because we both had fathers that beat our mothers senselessly. One day when I was eleven years old, I was coming out of the Projects, on my way to the playground at the end of the parking lot, when Juelz came off of the stairwell bleeding from the mouth. His right eye was busted, and he looked like he was about to pass out. He crashed into me. I tried my best to hold him up, but we both wound up falling to the dirty floor right on top of a bunch of used crack pipes.

"Juelz! Juelz! What's good, bruh? What the fuck happened?" I asked, starting to panic. And then I saw the bloody knife in his hand, wet and dripping fresh blood. That spooked me.

"Fuck." His father kicked opened the door of the stairwell, stumbled against the wall, and slid his back against it, leaving a trail of blood. He clutched his right hand to his left shoulder and acted as if he was trying to reach around to it. He groaned as he looked down the stairwell at me and Juelz. "You lil' bitch ass nigga. You gon' stab me!" He bounced from the wall and made his way down the case of stairs.

Juelz got to his feet with his eyes wide open. The knife still in his hand dripping. "I ain't scared of you no more, Daddy. I ain't scared of you no more. Do what you gon' do." Tears ran down his small face. His gray eyes stayed pinned on the man coming down the stairs. He clutched the knife tighter.

"Yo, Juelz, let's get the hell out of here, man. Come on. You can't fight your Pops. He crazy, man. Look at him," I said, eyeing the older man rushing down the steps with a menacing stare on his face.

"I'm finna kill you, lil' nigga. Then I'ma go back up there and kill that dope fiend ass bitch. Watch."

He was no more than ten steps away from reaching our landing. I started to panic. Grew worried. I didn't know what to do. I could tell that he was ready to do something drastic. He appeared drunk and high. His eyes were bucked and glossy. I'd seen those kind of eyes before on the many dope addicts that lived in our building and roamed our neighborhood. It seemed almost normal. But a part of me knew that it wasn't. I knew that there had to be more to life than the Cabrini Green Projects.

"Let's go, Juelz. Please, man. I don't want to see him hurt you. We're just kids, man." I tried to pull his arm, but he knocked it away and rushed toward his father with the knife in his hand, hollering a battle cry at the top of his lungs. His old man waited until he got close enough, then kicked him in the chest, causing him to fly back down the stairs and into me. We both crashed to the floor again. His elbow landed in my neck, making it hard for me to breathe for a few seconds.

Juelz's father picked him up with two hands and choked him as hard as he could. "You ungrateful lil' bastard. I told you I was gon' kill you, didn't I? Didn't I'?" He choked him harder and harder.

I could literally see my friend's face turning redder and redder. His eyes bugged out of his face with tears coming out of the ducts. I ran to his dad as fast as I could, swinging with all of my might, punching his big back. He had to weigh about 250 pounds. Solid muscle. He'd been released from Statesville Maximum Security Prison only three weeks prior, and already he was drinking heavily and smoking large quantities of crack cocaine. He appeared deranged and

40

overly angry. "Put him down, man! Put him down! You're killing him!" I hollered and continued to punch him as hard as my little fists would allow me to, but he seemed unaffected by the blows. He continued to choke Juelz, on his way to murdering him.

Now I really started to panic. I looked all around the area that we were in for a weapon. All I saw were plenty burnt crack pipes, syringes, and ropes that were used to tie around the heroin addict's arm so that a vein could appear more prominent. Empty bottles of liquor and dead rats. Seeing Juelz's face turn a shade of purple and his eyes roll into the back of his head, I knew that I had to move fast. Up against the wall was a St. Ides forty ounce bottle. I rushed over to it and pull it out of the brown paper bag that was covering it. Grabbed it by the top end and rushed back over to Juelz's father who was nearly finished with killing him. Jogged up three stairs past them, situated myself, then jumped in the air and brought the bottle down on the top of his bald head, busting it wide open. *Bam!* It exploded in my hands.

"Argh!" He dropped Juelz and fell down the stairs. Blood rushed out of the wound on the top of his head and into his eyes. He crawled around on the floor looking disoriented. "Aw, now you done done it, muthafucka. Now I'm about to kill you and him. Wait till this dizzy shit wear off." He promised.

I pulled Juelz up and helped him to make it out of the hallway. We wound up running across the big parking lot in fear for our lives. Didn't come home until after the street lights came on that night. By that time, there were more than twenty police cars in front of our building, along with the black coroner's van. I guess after we'd run away from Juelz's father, the man had gone back upstairs and killed Juelz's mother by stabbing her more than fifty times. It was gruesome. After he killed her he attempted to rob a few drug dealers in our building but was unsuccessful. He was shot five times and found propped up against the front door of his apartment. The same apartment that he'd killed Juelz's mother in. Life was a bitch, but she always got her revenge.

* * *

Juelz pulled up in front of the Projects in a dark blue Chevy Caprice Classic with seventeen inch Daytons on them. The paint was clean. The rims were shining, and the interior was all white leather, had televisions in the headrests, and smelled like the little maple tree car fresheners. He jumped out of the whip and shook up with me. It was five o'clock in the afternoon, the day of Punkin's Sweet Sixteen party. "What it do, nigga?"

I shook up with him, gave him a side-hug, pat his back, then stepped backward. I was fitted in an all-platinum Rocawear denim get up, with a black and silver Raiders fitted cap that off-set my black and gray Space Jam Jordan's. Had a diamond stud in each ear, and a fresh haircut. My waves were thick and popping. I ain't have much hair on my face at this point, but my chin stubble was thick enough to be lined up, so it was. Both it and my mustache. I was even smelling good. Miss Jackie had taken good care of me. I had about four more fits in my closet too, with the Jordan's or Airmax to match.

Juelz looked me up and down. "Nigga, I know Kalvin ain't spitting out that kind of cream for you to be dressed like that. And Harold's ain't doing the trick either, so where you getting this scratch from? I want in." He adjusted the pistol in his waistband. I could see the handle sticking out.

"I put a few chips to the side so I could make sure that I looked up to par for Punkin's party. You know how it is. You rolling over there wearing that?" I asked, looking over his black Guess shorts and white T shirt. He was rocking a pair of all-white Nike Air Force Ones.

He looked down at himself. "Hell yeah. Shit, I'm straight. Besides, them bitches gon' wanna fuck this whip anyway. Look at them rims. Them bitches seventeen inches. Project Hoes trying to call me up to their roach-infested cribs already. Straight up. Let's roll out." He walked around the front of the car and mugged the area that we were parked in. There were people out everywhere. Females out pushing strollers up and down the block with other chicks walking alongside of them. They were next to nothing. Had little shorts on that were all up in their ass cracks. Some of them were smoking blunts, while others were talking on their phones. There were groups of niggas everywhere we looked. Some had their hats to the right, and some to the left. The ones that had their hats to the left were running under the Five Point Star. And the ones that were turned to the right were under the Six Point Star.

The five wore red and black, and the six wore blue and black. They were rival gangs and were serious about their crews. The Cabrini Green averaged at least two murders a day, and while that may not seem like much, keep in mind that the whole hood only expanded out about six blocks. So that was ridiculous. I also saw little girls jumping Double Dutch, and some little kids playing basketball on the courts not far from where we were. The sun was shining, and it had been a beautiful day so far. Nobody had gotten shot, but in my Projects, most of the killers didn't wake up until after five o'clock at night. That's when the bullshit started.

I held the handle on the new whip that Juelz was pushing. "Nigga, where you get this whip from? I need to know that before I even get in this ma'fucka." I looked over at him.

He was about six-feet even. Light skinned with gray eyes, and short naturally curly hair. Slim. His mother had been Puerto Rican, and his father Black and white. His eyes were tight, almost Asian like. He gave me a smile and opened the car door. "Aw, we good for at least twenty-four hours. I caught this bitch on my way back from Gary. Caught a nigga slipping at the rest stop, fucking with one of them hooker bitches. I waited until he was done, then followed him in the bathroom and smoked his bitch ass. Got three hunnit off of him, and about a ball of dope. He was broke. Wish

I had known that before I sent him on his way." He sat in the car and I just stood there. This made him look up at me. "What's good?"

"Bruh, you got me fucked up. You just said that you murked a nigga for this whip and robbed his ass. That's the death penalty. Looking fly ain't worth all of that. Hell n'all." I said, walking away from his dumb ass. I was about to get on the train and head to Punkin's crib that way. The train would get me there in fifteen minutes. It was my safest bet instead of fucking with Juelz's crazy ass. He was always smoking somebody for nothin'. I was sure the death of his peoples fucked him up.

He jumped out of the car and caught up to me. "TJ, bruh, trust me. We got at least twenty four hours, but for the sake of argument let's just use six hours, then I'ma get rid of this bitch. We gotta flex on some hoes though. Nigga, I'm sitting on seventeens. These bitches are gold. I'll even let you drive if you want to. Think about the effect you'll have on Punkin pulling up in this." He smirked and snickered.

I shot him a quick angry look. "Bruh, I don't even like shorty like that." I lied. "I'm fucking with Sodi. She way colder. Punkin fucking with that bum nigga Blue." I walked back to the car, past him and sat in the driver's seat. The seats were all leather. The car smelled so good. Even though I knew it was stupid, I had to drive this bad boy. Had to let Punkin see me rolling clean. I was sure to flex on every nigga at the party.

Juelz sat into the passenger's seat and let it all the way back. "Who you think you're fooling? You feeling shorty like a ma'fucka. Nigga, I be watching ya' eyes and shit. You can't keep them boys off of her. She is bad though. I gotta give you that. But Sodi cold, too. Plus, she Spanish. Spanish hoes crushing them Black bitches, easy." He took a blunt out of the ashtray and set fire to it. "I'd fuck with Sodi over Punkin any day."

I imagined my mother and my little sister. Thought about how beautiful they were to me, and how I felt that there wasn't a prettier woman walking the face of this earth than my mother. I got irritated. "Nigga, you got the game fucked up. Spanish bitches ain't got shit on the Black sistas. All they is, is pretty in the face. That's it. Sistas be pretty in the face, bodies be cold, and they be jazzier than a rich bitch on her period."

Juelz sucked his teeth. "Yeah the fuck right. Spanish bitches got everything. They got the hair. The eyes. The body. And they be cooking up a storm. Not to mention their fingernail and toe game be on point. Most Black bitches be neglecting their fingers and toes. That's whack. And they be rocking weave 'cause they shit don't grow that far. Spanish bitches be natural. Born tine. Black hoes be buying fake hair to look like them." He took a pull of the blunt and blew the smoke to the ceiling.

I was sitting in the driver's seat steaming as I weaved through traffic. I thought about how my sister's hair was well past her shoulders, and how my mother's fell to the top of her back. They both rocked weave every now and then, but I didn't see a problem with that, or when any female did. In fact, to me it was normal. I felt like Juelz was flexing on my race of women and that made me wanna elbow him in the face.

"Damn, nigga, you quiet as hell. I hit yo ass with that sauce about them Black hoes huh? You can't get up?" He snickered. "That truth hurts." He handed me the blunt after dumping it in the ashtray.

I took it and pulled off of it twice, inhaled, and took two more pulls, inhaled, another one, and passed it back to him, blowing smoke out of my nose thickly. I cracked the window. "Without no Africa, there is no Spain, or Spanish women, period. Puerto Ricans, Cubans, Dominicans, and all of that are only fine like they are because they have our

Black blood in them. Those islands were used as slave trading posts for the White man back in the day. We were also dropped off on those islands to take care of the sugar cane, tobacco, and cotton fields. Once there, your men and women mated with the locals. Years and years later, their population got finer, but only 'cause we dipped in their race pool. Let's get that straight. Ain't no race pure. You gon' find Black in anything that is beautiful. Even yo' Puerto Rican, mixed up ass got the Mother Land in you, or else you'd be an ugly, funny looking ass nigga more than you already are," I spat, and mugged him, half-playing and half serious. I needed us to switch the subject before my temper got the best of me.

Me and Juelz had gotten into more than fifty fights since we had been friends and I felt another one brewing on my end. I couldn't help seeing my mother and sister whenever he took shots at my race of women. I couldn't help it.

He blew smoke out of his nose and looked over at me. "Aiight, let's get off of this subject because I can see your nostrils flaring and all type of shit. Let's just get to the party and fuck with these bitches. Here." He handed me back the blunt and I agreed.

Chapter 5

Sodi almost broke her neck to get around to the driver's side just as I was stepping out of the stolen whip, with the sun dancing off the top of my waves. I felt fresher than a pair of new shoes. I opened my arms and she ran inside of them, hugging me tight. "Damn, Papi, you showed up to show out, didn't you?" She looked over the car and then back up to me. She had her long, curly hair dropped past her waist. She was rocking a tight fitted Chanel dress over Chanel three inch heels. Her toes were painted with little C's in them, along with her fingernails. She had pink diamond earrings in her ear and a matching chain around her neck that read, *Sodi*. All in all, she was bad; crushing shit.

I looked over to Juelz and he gave me a look as he nodded that said he was right, and I couldn't lie.

She stood on her tippy toes and kissed my lips with her eyes closed. I could taste the Cherry Blossom painted over them. After the kiss, she grabbed my hand and pulled me toward the party. "Come on, Papi. I wanna flex on these hoodrats with you. They ain't never seen you cleaned up like this. Plus, I want them to see what you're rolling."

Juelz waved me off. "Gon' head, Boss. I'll fuck with you in a minute. I see a couple hoes from school that I wanna get up with. I'll meet y'all inside later." He jogged off and caught up with a pretty Brazilian chick that had just transferred to our school from Miami. She was golden complexed with her long hair in a pony tail down her back. She was fitted in a Prada dress that was hugging her like a second skin.

I nodded in approval, then Sodi grabbed my chin, and tilted it down to her. "Damn, Papi, she fine, but I am too. Can I get a little attention? You just got here." She looked into my eyes. Little crinkles formed across her forehead. Her juicy lips were shining bright. She smelled good.

I nodded. "My bad, baby. Shorty is bad though. But you doing ya' thing, too. Let's roll." I threw my arm around her and we went up the steps on our way inside the party.

It was so crowded outside that it looked like she'd invited the whole school to attend her birthday bash. The day before, I'd spent $400 on a diamond tennis bracelet from Jared's and I was hoping that it was a good enough gift for Punkin. I could only imagine how many she would get. I just wanted mine to stand out more than everybody else's.

We stepped into the packed living room. The sun was just going down, but already people were getting their groove on, on the dance floor, grinding to a Nicki Minaj track. We weaved our way through them, further into the house. It seemed that most of the females there were damn near naked. I couldn't concentrate on Sodi even though she was under my arm. She kept on looking up at me annoyed. I couldn't help it. I'd never seen so many big, exposed asses in one place, at one time. The music was so loud that I couldn't hear myself think. There was a flickering disco light that made it feel like we were walking in slow motion. Finally, we made our way into the kitchen. Punkin stood over a table, pouring juice into a bunch of cups. Her mother Linda helped her. I couldn't believe how fine Punkin looked.

She had on a big, pink Cindrella-like dress with a crown on her head that had pink diamonds in it. Her hair was in thick curls. They were shiny and full of sheen. She had this real cute glitter all over her face that made her look mystical. She wore fake eyelashes, but they looked good. Her makeup was on fleek, just like the rest of her ensemble. I even peeped her toe game, and they were perfectly pedicured, painted to match her dress. She got my stamp of approval.

I made eye contact with her. She smiled at first, then looked down at Sodi and frowned. I took my arm from around her and stepped over to the birthday girl, just as she handed some dark skinned chick a drink. "Happy Sweet Sixteen, Goddess." I held my arms open for her to come inside.

She pursed her lips and rolled her eyes. "Un-huh." She stepped into my embrace and hugged me. She smelled so good that I was sure I held her for too long. Her body felt so soft and ample. I felt like scooping her off and putting some of that Miss Jackie Teachings on her.

Sodi grabbed my arm. "Awright, that's enough. Dang. You still my date." She pulled me away and stepped in front of me, placing her back on my chest. "Girl, he rolled to your party in a hooked up whip. It got gold rims and everything. Like it's been pimped or something. I can't wait to roll in it."

Punkin looked up at me and frowned. "Wonder where you got that from. We don't make that much money at Harold's." She rolled her eyes and bumped past me. "Thanks for coming, TJ."

I watched her disappear into a crowd. I felt sick. Wanted to chase her, but Sodi's clingy ass wasn't trying to let me break free of her.

Linda, Punkin's mother, made eye contact with me and smiled. She looked like an older yet still real fine version of her daughter. "Are you thirsty, baby?"

I looked her up and down and shook my head. "No, thank you, ma'am, but if you need help preparing the drinks for everybody I wouldn't mind giving you a hand." I offered, trying anyway I could to get rid of Sodi for a second. I also wanted to pick Linda's brain. I was curious about Punkin.

Sodi turned around to face me. "No, you can't help. I been waiting to see you all day. Now that you're here, you're going to spend some time with me. Come on, we're gonna dance." She grabbed my arm and led me into the party.

I wanted to yank my shit away, but that mean streak wasn't in me yet. I tried to be respectful and understanding to all females at this point. I'd grown up in a household where the women in my family where so undervalued, demoralized, disrespected, and verbally and physically assaulted. Their feelings were ignored on a daily basis. That stuck in my heart like an arrow from Cupid. So, when I interacted with other females I always kept their feelings at the forefront of my brain.

Linda smiled. "Looks like you got a handful to deal with. Y'all have fun, baby. Later."

We made it to the living room and found us a nice spot, even though there was barely any room. Sodi got in front of me and rubbed her ass all in my lap. I could feel her crack and everything. I trailed my hands up and down her hips. All the way up to her small breasts. Cuffed them, then rubbed back down her body. She was making me feel some type of way.

She turned to me and we started tonguing each other down. I rubbed all over her ass. Squeezing it and sliding my hand into the space between her legs from the back. Rubbing until I felt her soft kitty lips. They felt puffy. She moaned into my ear while I played with them through her dress. "Ay, Papi. I'ma give you some tonight. I'm supposed to spend a night at Punkin's house, but we can go somewhere and do our thing. Her mother works third shift tonight, too. But I'm down."

I gripped that ass and pulled her closer to me. "Sound good to me. I been wanting to hit this pussy anyway. See if you can handle Papi, nah'mean?" I sucked her bottom lip, gripped that ass tighter, then turned her back around so she could twerk in my lap. I loved when females did that. And she was good at it too. She found a way to locate my pole, then jerked it up and down while she grooved in her own sexy way.

I kissed all over her neck. Had her ear lobe in my mouth when I looked across the room and made eye contact with Punkin. Blue had his arms around her waist. Every time he tried to cuff her ass, she knocked his hands away and scolded him. She turned her nose up at me and looked off. Once again, I felt sick. I didn't know what I'd done to make her so angry. I was thinking that maybe she was mad because she thought that I hadn't bought her a gift when I really had. I figured I'd just wait until the song ended then give it to her. But Sodi wasn't ready to leave off of the floor after only dancing to one song. We wound up staying on it for a full hour. By that time, I was tired of dancing and ready to fuck her lil' ass.

I leaned down and placed my lips to her ear. "Yo, Sodi, I'm trying to hit this pussy right now. Let's go out to the car real quick." I sucked her earlobe into my mouth. My dick was so hard that it hurt.

She moaned. "Baby, what's the matter? You can't wait until later on tonight? Aren't you enjoying the party?" She pressed her booty back into my lap.

The length of me squeezed between her cheeks. That only made me hornier. "Hell n'all, I can't. I need some of this body right now, or I'm about to bounce. Straight up." I was thinking of hitting up Miss Jackie so I could get some of that vet pussy. It seemed like she knew how to work my lil' young ass, and I was getting better at hitting her pussy too. Besides, it was getting to the point that every time I fucked her that she always had some kind of gift for me. Gifts that I used to help out at home, and whatever was left over I'd use on myself. Home came first though.

Sodi turned around to face me. "Dang, you gon' do me like that?"

I looked off and saw Punkin walking toward the back of the house. Blue looked like he was angry about something. "Yo, I don't want to, but I'm all riled up now. I gotta find a way to calm down. I'll check with you later." I stepped around her and headed toward the front door. I was about to call Miss Jackie for a quickie. My mind was made up. Before I could even reach the door though, Sodi caught up and grabbed my arm. I looked down on her. "What's good, man? I said I check with you later."

Linda squeezed past us and headed toward the front door with a big bag draped over her shoulder. She was dressed in scrubs. "Sodi, I'm trusting y'all. This party is to end at ten o'clock. The Jacksons from next door will be stopping over at nine thirty to make sure of that. I've already talked to Punkin, now I'm talking to you. Y'all don't let me down." She hugged her and stepped off of the porch. I watched her big booty jiggle as she made her way to her Benz truck. I didn't even know that she was so thick. That was hot to me.

"TJ, we can fuck later. But if you can't wait, I can at least give you some head to tie you over. Is that cool?"

I wanted some pussy. Head was good, but there was nothing like pussy to me. I was obsessed with a female's scent while I was hitting that shit. But since I was so horny from her rubbing up against me, I took her up on her offer. "Yeah, it's good. Come on, I'ma let you suck me up in the whip, that way you can feel like a Boss bitch or what not." I grabbed her hand.

We made our way through the crowds and to the car, but when we got there, Juelz was already in the backseat letting the Brazilian chick ride him with the top of her dress pulled down. Her dark brown nipples stood out proudly as she bounced up and down on him with her mouth wide open. The sight of her made my dick harder. I opened the driver's side door, and popped the lock for Sodi to get in. She put up a fight at first but gave in after two minutes. After a few seconds in the car, she had my piece in her mouth, giving me the business. I pulled down the top of her dress so I could play with her titties while she slobbed me up and drove me crazy. She wasn't a beast like Miss Jackie, but the potential was definitely there. I just had to work with her a lil' bit. Help her practice. I had my fingers tangled into her curly hair, humping into her mouth. My eyes were in the rearview mirror, peeping the Brazilian, Mandy, though.

Shorty was super fine to me. Our eyes locked and she pulled her dress further down to really show me her titties. She had her back to Juelz's chest, riding him slowly. When she reached between her legs and opened her pussy lips, I was thankful that the car was parked under a street lamp and I could see that. I came down Sodi's throat, groaning, imagining that I was fucking Mandy.

I pulled out of her mouth and kissed Sodi on the forehead. "Good job, baby."

She wiped her lips and smiled. "You're welcome, Papi. We'll finish tonight, I promise."

We headed back into the party, and it was still juking. I saw plenty broads on their knees twerking hard with their dresses pulled up on their backs. Thongs splitting their ass cheeks. I felt like I was in heaven. Had to piss though and told Sodi I'd meet her in the living room after I finished. She reluctantly let my arm go and made me promise that I'd be right back, which I did, Even though I wanted to shake her ass. I wanted to find Punkin. She was the whole reason I'd come to the party in the first place. I went into the bathroom, pissed, and used one of the towels in there to wash my privates. Washed the towel back out and tossed it in the hamper. Checked my wave game in the mirror, saw that I was popping, and stepped back into the party when Blue flew past me along with Punkin. He had her by the arm all aggressive and shit. Drug her to the back room and tossed her inside before slamming the door.

I heard him use the bitch word a bunch of times. Then a loud ass smack. More bitches, then two smacks. Punkin yelped and begged for him to stop. Then he was snapping out again. He was hollering so loud that I could hear him clearly over the music. They were in a back room that was connected to the kitchen. It seemed like nobody was paying attention to the altercation other than me. I became heated. Having flashbacks of my father kicking my mother's ass for no reason. That year he'd beat her on her birthday just because he felt like it. I felt a sudden case of deja vu. I became infuriated, especially when another slap sounded.

Juelz showed up behind me, smelling like weed and pussy. "What's good, nigga? You want one of these pills?"

He asked with his arm around Mandy. Her hair was all over the place now. Even her makeup was smudged.

I knew that Blue's older brothers were plugged. They ran under the Six Point Star, were gangsters, and had plenty pull on the northwest side of Chicago. Getting into it with him would mean a lot of drama for myself so I had to tip toe that line. "N'all, maybe later. Yo, you got that banger on you?" I asked eyeing the door knob to the back room. Two more slaps sounded. I got more and more heated. My mother's beatings flashed through my mind's eye.

Juelz sucked his teeth. "Nigga, is that even a question?" He took out a Glock .40 and handed it to me. "What's good?"

I put the pistol on my waist, and grabbed the knob, twisting it. Pushing in the door, I found Blue on top of Punkin between her legs with her dress pushed up to her chest. There was blood on the white sheet by her head. I couldn't see her face because the dress was blocking it. His pants were below his waist. He looked like he was just about to slide into her.

I snapped. I don't know why I did, but I did. I wrapped my arm around his throat and drug him off of her, forcing him to the floor. "Fuck you in here doing to her, nigga?" I watched Punkin scoot to the headboard and pull her dress down. Tears were all over her face. Her nose was bloodied. Her eyes wide open in shock. Reminders of my mother came to me once again.

Blue hopped up and pulled his pants up. "This ain't got shit to do with you, nigga. Fuck you all in my business fo?" He spat.

One glance to Punkin, seeing the blood dripping off of her lip, and I lost it. I punched him right in the nose and snapped it. Then hit his ass with a right hook that made his face crash into the wall. From there he dropped to one knee. "Bitch ass nigga, do me like that. Rape me, fuck nigga. What's good?" Grabbed the back of his head and slammed my knees into his face with all of my might. That knocked his ass out cold. He lay on the carpet; blood dripping from his mouth and nose.

I wanted to finish him off, but Juelz grabbed me. "Nigga, come on. Let's get the fuck out of here. That's a bunch of drama right there. Fuck." He snapped, pulling me toward the exit of the room.

People were coming to see what all of the commotion was about. I jerked away from him and climbed across the bed to Punkin. "Ma, you good? Can I do anything to help you?" I asked. I wanted to console her and to help her in any way that I could like I always tried to do with my mother.

She shook her head wildly and scooted away from me. Her eyes were bucked. She looked afraid and out of her mind. Every time I made a move to touch her, she freaked out.

"Yo, come on, TJ. One of them bitches just called that nigga brother. You know he plugged. Let's bounce before we have to kill something!" He rushed out of the room.

I stood there for a brief moment, stuck. Finally, I went into my pocket and tossed the diamond tennis bracelet next to her before I rushed to catch up with Juelz. Sodi screamed my name as we jumped into the car. As soon as I tossed the keys to Juelz, he threw them into the ignition and peeled away from the curb.

We rolled in silence for nearly the whole trip home, then he spoke up. "Yo, that's some beef that we don't want. Then niggas are Folks. So is half of Chicago. I don't care about killing Blue, but we can't kill all of them before they kill us. Damn. I knew that bitch was gon' be trouble. Yo, she ain't got shit on Sodi. You should have just worried about her. Now we gotta deal with this shit."

I kept my mouth closed and looked out of the window. The fear in Punkin's eyes when it came to me weighing heavy on my heart. I was questioning if I had done the right thing. I ain't feel like arguing with Juelz so I just let him talk. My mind was somewhere else.

* * *

When I stepped into the house that night, Marie was kneeling in front of my mother, dabbing her face with a warm cloth. My mother's face was swollen worse than I had ever seen it before. Both of her eyes were nearly closed. She had a cast on each arm.

Marie looked up at me with tears in her eyes. "He wouldn't stop beating her, TJ. He just wouldn't stop." She whimpered.

My mother looked up at me and tried her best to smile. That broke my heart. I felt like I was about to throw up. "Hey, baby. Don't be mad. I'm okay." She slurred, but I knew it was a lie. Tears fell from my eyes.

"Where is he at, Mama? Where is that nigga at?" I wanted to know.

"He upstairs at Rebecca house. They up there doing that dope. I hope you kick his ass, TJ. Seriously." Marie cried.

Chapter 6

I beat on the door with the butt of the .40 Glock. My teeth were clenched together. Brows furrowed. I waited a few seconds then banged again, this time harder than before. I could smell the crack cocaine smoke inside of the hallway. I didn't know if it was coming from out of Rebecca's apartment, or from somebody else's. I got my answer seconds later when the door swung inward, and a cloud of the stanky ass smoke poofed into my face.

Rebecca's eyes were big as paper plates. Her hair was nappy and all over her head. The area under her eyes were sunken in and black. Her lips were white and crusty. Chapped, with a trace of blood on the bottom one. She wore a white T-shirt with Kool Aid stains on it. Her nipples pressed against the material. Her breasts were flat, saggy. She smelled like must and fish ss if she'd made a perfume using both fragrances. "What the fuck you doing beating on my door like you crazy, TJ? Yo daddy trying to relax."

That was all the knowledge I needed. I grabbed a handful of her hair and tossed her into the hallway. Slammed the door and locked it. She started to beat on it like she'd lost her damn mind. I scanned the roach and rat-infested house until I found my pops sitting at the table naked, with a pipe in his hand. A can of Old English in front of him. He had a long scratch along the side of his face. Probably from my mother trying to fight him off. I didn't know, and I didn't care. I made my way to the table and sat down across from him.

He picked up the pipe and set fire to the rock inside of it. Pulled until his jaws hollowed out. Then inhaled and held the smoke before blowing it across the table and into my face. Then he frowned. "Fuck you want, lil' bitch nigga?" He curled his lip.

I took the pistol off of my hip and slammed it on the table so hard that it knocked his beer and a plate of dope that was in front of him off.

He stood up. "Boy, if you don't get yo' monkey ass out of here, I'ma beat you like I did that bitch. Not get! And Rebecca, quit beating on that damn door for I kill you!" he hollered past my shoulder.

I remained seated, Mugging him with hatred. "Why you do my mother like that, Kalvin?" I felt the beats of my heart speeding up.

"What? Boy, if you don't get yo' ass out of here." I grabbed the gun and slammed it on the table again.

"I said why you do my mother like that, Kalvin! I'm not gon' ask you again. Nigga, what's good? Speak!"

"Speak? You lil' pussy ass nigga. On my Five you ain't talking that shit to me. I'm yo' daddy. And she my bitch. If I wanna--"" Was all he managed to get out of his mouth.

I grabbed the gun, and flipped the table. With lighting speed smacked him across the face with the weapon. His head jerked backward. Before he could absorb that blow, I beat the pistol into his face four more times and stood up. "Get yo punk ass up. Come on, nigga." I put the gun on safety and tucked it into my pocket. I ain't need no pistol to beat this coward. I was gon' handle him like a man. Like something he was not, and had never been.

Only a coward could beat the mother of his children the way that he did. I hated his fucking guts. Images of my mother's face played like a DVD in my mind.

He stood up and put his guards up. Two knots already formed on his forehead. "Aw, nigga, you finna have to kill me. I spit you out of my dick. Not the other way around." He rushed me like a professional boxer, protecting his chin. Threw a jab, and caught me in the jaw, then a left hook that I blocked, but his right jab caught me again. My old man was a southpaw boxer. Meaning that his power hand was his left. He lead with his right to set you up so his left could finish you.

I boxed the same way and fucked niggas over on a regular because of this. I stumbled backward and caught my footing. Tried to calm myself. When I got mad fighting, every blow I threw was with power, and not thought out. That would get anyone's ass whooped.

Fighting was more mental than physical. It was like a game of Chess that hurt when you made the wrong move. In order to whoop Kalvin, I had to outthink him. Be smart, or he would reign victorious over me and whoop me just as he had my mother. So, I regained my footing and protected my chin. He swung a haymaker, I side-stepped him, grabbed that pistol back out of my waist, said fuck that, and smacked him along the side of the head. He hollered and fell to one knee.

I cracked him again, splitting him open. Blacked out, hitting over and over again. "You. Pussy. Ass. Nigga. Keep. Your. Hands. Off. Of. My. Mother. Don't. You. Touch. Her. Again." I shouted, fucking him over. I didn't come to until I noticed that he was unmoving. This made me back up and go into a state of panic. He laid on his side with blood gushing out of his face, and head. I rushed out of Rebecca's apartment, down her hallway toward the stairwell. I heard her scream in the background. I knew she had found my father on her floor twisted.

When I got back upstairs to our apartment, Marie was helping my mother put on her coat. They were on their way to the hospital. She took one look at me, saw the blood all over my face, and her eyes got bucked. "Did you kill him, TJ? Is that monster finally out of our lives?" Marie asked excitedly.

I shrugged. "I don't know. I think so. I just need to kiss my mother. Need to kiss my baby." I slowly pulled her into my arms and kissed all over her face with tears running out of my eyes. "Come on, Mama, I'ma get you out of here. I gotta take care of you. You're my angel." I kissed her some more, then took a hold of her hand.

She yanked it away. "TJ, Please tell me you didn't hurt him. Tell me you didn't hurt my husband," she pleaded, dropping to her knees and looking down at the carpet. There were specks of blood all over the beige carpet. When she looked back at me, she winced in pain, placed her fingers to her jaw and cried harder.

Marie kneeled beside her and rubbed her back. I stood there feeling like a damn fool. My heart hurt. I couldn't believe that she was reacting in such a way. After all I had done what I had for her honor. How couldn't she see that? "Mama, you should have known sooner or later that TJ was going to snap out. He's the only male in our family that loves you the right way. Neither Deion nor JD care about either one of us. I'm glad he did what he did. Kalvin deserves whatever happened." She continued to rub her back.

I looked down on her for moment, then offered to help her to her feet. She smacked my hand away and buried her face in Marie's chest. "Just go, TJ. Get out of here. I don't know what you did, but that's your father. You are never supposed to hurt him. Honor thy mother. Honor thy father. It's right there in the Bible. Lord, this family will never be blessed if we continue to sin against Jehovah." She slurred.

Now I was steaming mad. Heated. I couldn't believe that she would even speak in my father's honor after what he'd done to her. My mother's face was unrecognizable. She looked horrible, all because of his fists. "But who is honoring you, mama? Huh? Who is taking care of you? Huh!" I hated raising my voice at my Queen, but my mind was blown. How could she be so protective of this loser? So stubborn. I was so vexed that I didn't know what to do. I felt like I needed to get out of that apartment though before I said something that would emotionally bruise her.

I hustled to my room, grabbed a book bag and stuffed some of my good clothes inside of it. The ones that Miss Jackie had helped me to buy. Reached into the side of my mattress and grabbed the remainder of my money that I kept hidden there, when I heard the door bust open, and a bunch of groaning. I pulled out my pistol after placing the backpack on and rushed into the living room. My mother screamed at the top of her lungs along with Marie.

My father was face down on the floor with blood leaking from him. Rebecca stood in the hallway with her cell phone to her ear. I could tell that she was talking to the police because she was telling them what had happened and giving them our address. I watched my mother crawl over to my father. She was crying so loud that I could barely hear myself think.

Marie jumped up and ran to me. "TJ, get the hell out of here. That bitch calling the cops on you. When they see how you did him, they're going to lock you up. Please, just go." She hugged me, then kissed me on the cheek, pushing me toward the door.

"Why? Why, TJ? Why would you do this to him? He didn't deserve this. You're supposed to honor your father. He' not perfect but he didn't deserve this." She cried.

I made my way out of the door. I could hear him struggling to breathe. His head had swollen up to the size of a pumpkin. There were big knicks all over it with blood coming out of them. I didn't care how many wounds he had on him. I was in a fuck that nigga mode. The only thing that I cared about was the fact that his head was slightly bigger than my mother's. And both of his eyes were closed just as hers were. She was able to see out of hers just a tad, but his shit was closed shut. There was no peeking. I wished I could have patted myself on the back because I would have. I started to step over him on my way out of the door when I kneeled and kissed my mother. She pushed me away and said that she hated me. I felt sick to my stomach.

Marie looked on with a face of empathy for me, then waved me off. "Go, TJ. Please. Just go. We'll be okay."

I nodded and rushed out of the door. Rebecca jumped in my way and tried to grab me. "Oh, no you don't. I don't know where you think you're going but you're not going anywhere. You're going to wait here until the police come." She grabbed a handful of my shirt right by the collar, scratching me with her dirty nails. I felt them sting me right away.

Before I could say anything, Marie was in the hallway with a scowl on her face. "Don't be putting your hands on my brother!" She cocked back and punched Rebecca so hard in the face that she flew into the broken elevator doors. Hit the back of her head on the metal and fell to her ass. Sleep. Marie looked down on her and curled her upper lip. "I hate that bitch. Gon' now, big bruh. I'll call you when I find out what's going to take place with all of this." She hugged me again and stepped back. I could see her eyes watering.

Juelz appeared at the end of the hallway with a bag of Taco Bell. He smiled when he saw me. Gave me a whut up nod and headed in my direction. "Nigga, what's good? Why the fuck you ain't answering your phone? I just got a call from one of my old heads. I need you to bust this move with me."

The door opened to the stairwell, and Deion and JD came rushing out of it, into our apartment, nearly knocking Juelz over. "Aw, hell n'all!" Deion hollered. "What the fuck happened to him?" He asked trying to turn my father over so he could see his face. He didn't pay any attention to my mother's condition. He appeared numb to it.

I jogged toward Juelz. "Yo, let's get the fuck out of here. I had to touch my Pops up. His bitch called the police. I'm pretty sure they're on their way." I said looking over my shoulder.

Deion ran into the hallway. "Bitch ass nigga, you did this to our old man? What's good?"

JD came out and stood behind him. "Let's fuck this nigga up, big bruh. He always sticking his nose in our parents' business. Trying to save mama and shit. Come on." He broke into a sprint, headed in my direction. Both of his fists balled. Deion in tow.

I dropped my book bag and threw up my guards. As soon as he got close to me I rocked him with my right fist and smacked the shit out of him with my left. JD was a pussy. That nigga couldn't box. I didn't know how he survived in the Projects for as long as he did. But it wasn't because of his hand game, which is why he started to play with them toys real heavily at the age of fifteen. He flew into the wall and didn't get back up. Deion rushed me and caught me three times in the face. Fucked me up. I staggered and threw my guards up, but I was a bit dizzy. So, he rushed me and delivered blows everywhere he could until Juelz rocked his ass in the ear, picking him up and dumping him on his back so hard that I felt the floor vibrate.

"Let's get the fuck out of here, nigga." Juelz grabbed my arm, and we made our way to the stairwell door when Deion started busting back to back at us.

Boom. Boom. Boom. His bullets slammed into the wall and the door, creating sparks. Me and Juelz fled down the stairs, four at a time, until we got out of the building. By that time, I could barely breathe. My chest hurt.

* * *

That night I slept over Juelz's crib. I had a hard time digesting everything that had taken place with my family. I felt like the black sheep. Like I didn't have nobody in that household other than my sister, and that hurt because my mother was my life. I didn't know how to protect her. I didn't know what she expected from me, or what a son was supposed to do when his mother was in an impossible situation like the one my mother was in. I felt helpless. On top of that, no matter how much she appeared to fight the process, I was dead set on freeing her from my father's binds. I didn't know how I was going to do it, but I knew that I was. I had to free my sister as well. I could only imagine what happened behind the scenes between her and my father. She was growing up way too fast, and it burdened my soul to even think about what role my father played in that. I didn't get to sleep until about three in the morning that night. Juelz woke me up at around two-thirty, saying that he was going to bust a move. That he would be back first thing in the morning.

We shook up, and then I was out like a light. I dreamed of seeing my mother in a cemetery. I saw my father digging her grave before he tossed her body into it. Then he was dumping dirt onto her body with a big ass smile on his face. On the side of him was Marie. She lay on the ground half-dead. Struggling to breathe. He looked over at her. Picked up the shovel and got ready to bring it down onto her face, when I woke up hollering. My eyes were still closed tight. I felt sweat drip from my chin. I was drenched. I opened my eyes and was met by a room full of police officers.

They had their guns drawn, with their hammers cocked back. "Thylonius Jahrome Edwards, don't move! You're under arrest for attempted murder, and assault with a deadly weapon."

Chapter 7

I grew up thinking that my Pops was a pussy my whole life. I didn't care how many niggas he had killed. The way he did my mother day in and day out made it so that I could never respect him, or any nigga like him. I ain't have no love in my heart for him because of the things that I'd witnessed, and I never thought that I could think any less of him. That was until he took the stand and testified against me. I was his sixteen year old son, and this nigga took the stand and made it, so the judge and jury wanted to bam my ass. I ain't gon' get into everything he told them, but the end result was for the judge to sentence me to the State of Illinois Juvenile Prison System until I was eighteen years old. That was a year and eight months. I was devastated. Not only was I a bit fearful because of what I'd heard about St. Charles, or what we referred to in Chicago as the Gladiator School, but I worried about family support. I was already told that when you got locked up, if you didn't have any family to look out for you, that your bid was going to be real hard.

I already knew that my family was dirt poor, and on top of that with the exception of my sister, none of them cared about me. So, I knew it was going to be rough. Knowing this, I came into St. Charles with a fuck the world attitude. My first day at the prison I got into a fight with two dudes for the way they looked me up and down as if I was a female or something. One of the niggas licked his lips and blew a kiss at me. This was around dinner time. Both dudes were dark skinned and real heavy set, with big arms as if all they did was lift weights all day. To the average sixteen year old they would have been intimidating, but not me. I was on some kamikaze shit. I needed to feel some physical pain that would take me away from the emotional pain in my heart. So instead of side-stepping this gesture, I politely set my tray on the table in the cafeteria and dumped the food from it onto the table. Picked up the tray and headed back to the front of the chow hall where the two dudes were handing out napkins and milk. The one that was handing out milk had been the one to blow a kiss at me.

I felt I needed to check that shit out the gate. I wasn't with none of that gay shit. I didn't give a fuck what other niggas did, but it wasn't for me. When I approached the one handing out the milks, he looked down on me like I wasn't on nothing. "Say bruh, did you just blow a kiss at me?" I asked feeling the beats of my heart increase.

He smiled. "Hell yeah. I like what I see, and I see me fucking you before the week out. I run this shit here."

His guy handing out the napkins laughed. "If he fuck, I am too." They shook up and looked me up and down.

That was all it took. I snapped. I cocked back the tray and smacked the shit out of the milk server with it, then punched the napkin dude so hard in the throat that I felt my fist enter into the soft cushions of his neck. He started to gag and fell to his knees holding his throat. I grabbed him by the back of the head and brought my knee to his face twice. Then tackled his guy into the other meal trays. We fell over the counter. I straddled his bitch ass and pounded him with blow after blow. I was trying to fuck him up. I didn't understand how a nigga could be gay. And I especially didn't get how they thought that I was about to let them touch me in anyway.

I didn't know if there were more of them around this prison, but I was finna nip this shit in the bud right here. So, I fucked him up royally. Beat him so bad that they wound up throwing me in the hole for six months with no contact to anybody else. At first I thought I was going to go crazy. My room consisted of three white brick walls and a blue metal door with a window that was covered from the outside. There was a slab of concrete with a thin mattress on it. A toilet and sink that was attached to each other; both metal. No mirror, and a cement floor, that was it. The guards came around six times a day. Three times to give you your meal tray, and three times to pick them up. You were fed through a rectangular slot in the middle of the door. There was a long bright light at the top of the ceiling, and mine didn't work. There were roaches everywhere, and an occasional mouse. I didn't know how they got in, but they did.

The first three weeks were the worst for me. I kept hearing other niggas crying for their mother or swearing that they were going to kill themselves. In a six month period, eleven cats did. There were other dudes that cell boxed back and forth with each other. Cell boxing is when you argue threw the door for hours on end. I didn't take part in none of that shit, but there were many days that I got through off listening to them do it. I had never been the one to threaten a nigga before I whooped his ass. I didn't give warnings. I was the element of surprise type of nigga. I felt that if I could catch you off guard that I could win every time. I hated losing. Instead of allowing my situation to break me, I worked out religiously until my body gave up on me. Then I would grab my Bible and study. It didn't start off as studying, at first I just wanted something to read because I was so fucking bored. But then I began trying to understand the Bible on a deeper level. I didn't understand why God would allow for man to go through so many trials and tribulations.

How He'd allow for my mother to be beaten into the ground the way that she had been my entire life. How He'd curse us and allow for us to be raised in the Projects. No matter how much I read, I couldn't find the answers to these questions, so I put the Bible down and picked up the Qu'ran, but for me it was more of the same. I didn't get either book. We were given fifty sheets of paper and a pen insert once a week, every week, and a stamped envelope. I would always use the two sheets of paper to write Miss Jackie. She had been the only one holding me down. She made sure that I kept a few pennies on my books and had somewhere to call when the phone was offered to me once a month. Usually during those phone times I'd have her three way my sister, or my mother. Sometimes I'd even reach out to Sodi. She was writing me faithfully and sending me pics. But it was during this time in the hole that I began to write. I'd take the forty eight pages that were left over and write a short story. Then when I got bored the next day I'd reread what I had written, and this is how I entertained myself.

It got to the point that I couldn't wait for the paper to show up so I could take myself on a journey. Before I got out of the hole for that first six months, I had written over eighteen short stories. These stories were my lifelines because I honestly feel that had I not started to write I would have lost my freaking mind down there. About ninety-nine percent of the cats that went down to the hole emerged from it on some type of psychotropic medication. The prison staff had offered me medication on a few occasions, and I turned that shit down. I just didn't trust them and didn't feel weak enough to succumb. It didn't matter how hard I tried to be cool while I was in St. Charles Reformatory, I never stayed out of the hole for more than a few months at a time. I was always fighting. And when I fought I was trying to break shit because I knew how fucked up the hole was. I felt that if I was going to have to go down there for anything that it was going to be well worth it, so I always made sure that it was. I was fucking them niggas over there.

In addition to fighting and staying in the hole, I taught a lot of cats how to read and write. I also became an avid reader. I liked to study black history and things involving the Black woman. I needed to understand why my mother was set up the way that she was. Why she'd allow for my father to do her in the way that he did. I wanted to figure out how to help my sister to become all that she could. Every time I spoke to her on the phone she was always telling me about how things had gotten worse. How our father was doing heroin now. That Deion was a major player in the game, but that he also was doing heroin. JD was tooting powder cocaine and selling eight balls of crack. Rolling a Lexus truck, the same model as Deion's, but that neither one of them fuck niggas was looking out for her or my mother. She said she felt trapped and didn't know how much more she could take. This scared me. So, I tried to equip myself with as much knowledge as I could so that when I got home I could help her as much as I could.

About thirteen months into my bid, the prison came up with a theme called Family Intervention. It was when your family could come into the prison and spend eight hours with you. They'd be taken on a tour around the prison and during that time they could ask questions and be shown where you were kept, and all that kind of shit. They spoke with your social worker and were given updates about your well-being and rehabilitation. Afterwards, your people and another inmate's people would be grouped up and allowed to visit in a room away from everybody else's groups. The kicker was that the person who took part in this program had to be your mother, father, or adopted parent. Since my mother wasn't involved with me at all, and my old man was a loser, Miss Jackie signed up, and convinced them that she was my mother. This day she came with a picnic basket full of Gyros, Italian Beefs, Fried Chicken, deserts, and cold pops. After the tour we were led back to a small conference room where we were coupled with another family. The guards locked the door and said that they would be back in three hours.

Me and Miss Jackie set up our food and things on the other side of the room away from this light skinned nigga, his mother and sister-- I would later find out his girlfriend. Miss Jackie was fitted in a short purple Fendi skirt with a black and purple low-cut top. She rocked black Red Bottom heels and had her nails and toes done to match her fit. After she sat all of the food on the table, she pulled her chair alongside mine and looked around as if trying to locate a camera. But one of my chores for the prison was for me to clean the room we were in daily, so I knew that there was no camera or windows that we had to worry about. We were in the clear. And because the door didn't have a window on it either, there was no chance of us being surprised. If the guard came back we'd hear his key slipping into the lock.

She leaned over and kissed my neck. "Damn, I've missed you, TJ. Did you miss me?" She bit my neck and scooted closer to me.

I looked over her shoulder and saw that dude's mother was mugging us as if we lost our minds. I smiled and decided to play into what she already thought was a problem. Plus, I knew that it would turn Miss Jackie all the way on. "Yeah, mama, I missed you. I been thinking about you every single day. They be crapping on your son in here." I slid my hand up her waist and cupped her breast. Nudged her face to the side, then I was sucking and biting on her neck. My hand slid up her skirt. She was without panties. Her pussy was bald and hot. There was already dew on the lips. That excited me.

Dude's mother's eyes were bugged out of her head. She shifted uncomfortably in her chair and looked off. I slipped two fingers past Miss Jackie's lips and started to finger her fast. My dick throbbed in my pants. She struggled to get them down far enough so my piece could spring up. As soon as it did, her hand was around it pumping it. I sped up the pace between her legs. Her kitty was so wet that I could hear it.

"Hey!" Dude's mother yelled. "Ain't that your son?"

Miss Jackie nodded. "Yeah. Yeah. This my baby. Mind yo' business." She cocked her legs open wider so I could really dig into her. Then she stood up and straddled my lap. Hiked up her skirt, and grabbed my dick, forcing herself down on it. "Uh! Son!" She grabbed my shoulders and bounced up and down. Her hot pussy felt like a latex fist. The scent was glorious.

Looking over her shoulder I saw the face of dude's mother. She covered her daughter's eyes and got ready to jump up I assumed to get a guard when her son stopped her.

"Mama, no. I ain't trying to be labeled a snitch in here. That'll get me killed. Everybody just look this way." He ordered and helped her turn her chair away from us.

No lie, that had been his best move. Had he allowed his moms to snitch on me and Miss Jackie, I would have waited until I got out of the hole and shanked him up as soon as I could. What we were doing wasn't their business. Everybody in his circle appeared grown, even his girlfriend.

His sister, a high yellow chick with green eyes, moved his mother's hand from her eyes. "Hell n'all, mama, that's hot. I'm watching them. If they're brazen enough to do it in the open, then they should expect an audience. Besides, boy, you better smash this girl while you can." She pushed his girlfriend toward him.

He caught he and laughed. "Damn, mama, maybe you should look the other way." He pulled his girl onto his lap.

Miss Jackie bounced up and down with her head thrown back. Her pussy felt incredibly tight. I yanked down her top, and her big pretty titties spilled out. I sucked them, licking all over the mounds. Once again infatuated by the body of this older woman. The nipples stood up like erasers. She tasted like perfume at first, and then skin. I pushed them together and went crazy sucking and pulling on her nipples. I loved playing with her titties. I don't know why, but I just did.

She rode me faster and faster. "TJ! Son. I'm about to cum. I'm about to cum, baby. Uh. Shit!" She held the back of the chair and started to pop in my lap faster and faster. I felt her back lock up, and then she was cumming hard, licking the side of my face.

I stood her up and bent her over the table. Got behind her stroking my dick up and down. Then guided myself into her. Grabbed her hips, before ramming that wet box from the back. Her ass cheeks jiggled and shook. I grabbed a handful of her hair and sucked on her neck while I fucked in and out of her. From the corner of my eye I saw dude's mother slip her hand under her own skirt. Her back to her son and his girlfriend as they did their thing. Her hand moved back and forth. She bit into her lip and moaned, watching us attentively. This made me step my game up.

I smacked Miss Jackie on the ass hard. "Give me this pussy, mama! This mine! Tell me it's mine!"

"Uh! It's yours, baby. It's yours." She slammed backward into me. Her cheeks were like Jell-O.

I rubbed all over them and ran my thumb in circles around her anus. It constantly winked at me. I wanted to fuck it so bad. When I saw dude's, mother yank her skirt backward, slip her hand into her panties and began to finger herself fast and hard, I came in Miss Jackie. Squirt after squirt.

"Uh! Baby, I feel you cumming in me. Shit, it feel so good." She whimpered and continue to slam into my lap until I was back super hard.

Because I knew that dude's sister and his mother was watching me, I pulled all the way out so they could see my glistening penis. The head looked like a crab apple I was so horny. His mother scooted forward on her fingers five times, screamed and came all over herself. I couldn't believe that she could even do that with her son in the room, but it didn't bother me. I thought it was hot to be honest.

His sister came over to us and stood right beside Miss Jackie. "Let me jump down with y'all. Please," she begged, reached and wrapped her hand around my dick, squeezing it.

Miss Jackie smacked it away. "Hell n'all. This ain't that type of party. You better go over there and give him some pussy. He look like he know how to fuck." She nodded at the other nigga that was in the room with us. He appeared to be fucking the shit out of his girlfriend. They were in the missionary with her legs wrapped around his waist.

The girl frowned. "What? That's my brother. I can't do that."

Miss Jackie blocked her. "Well, this is my son, and ain't nobody touching him but me." She dropped to her knees and slid me into her mouth again, as if to tease dude's sister and mother.

I made eye contact with his mother. She opened her legs wide and showed me her pussy. Peeled the lips apart so I could see her pink. It looked so good.

* * *

The rest of my stay at St. Charles consisted of me going in and out of the hole. Every time I went down there, I would write as many short stories as I could to entertain myself. By the time I left St. Charles I had over a hundred stories written.

Chapter 8

I got out in April on my eighteenth birthday. The sun was shining bright, and when I walked through the gates of the prison I was shocked to see that Miss Jackie had went and snatched up Sodi. She stood waiting by Miss Jackie's Porsche, in a colorful Prada sundress that blew in the wind. Her long, curly hair blew behind her. She shielded her eyes from the sun as I made my way toward them. I'd chosen to leave everything that I had accrued over my time in the prison, inside the prison. I gave away all of my clothes, food, my tablet, magazines. Everything. The only thing I kept was the short stories that I'd written. They were my family. Pieces of a broken me.

As soon as I cleared the gates, Sodi took off into a full sprint and jumped into my arms, hugging me tight. "Papi. Papi. You're free. I can't believe that you are free."

I held her up but looked over her shoulder at Miss Jackie. She kissed her hand and blew me a kiss. Got into her Porsche and waited for us to finish with our reunion. I set Sodi down. "Ma, I appreciate all of the pictures and the letters. That took a lot of maturity to do what you did so I owe you for that." I kissed her lips, slid my hands down and cuffed her ass. She'd gotten a lot thicker since I had been away. Her face was a bit fuller. In my opinion she was ten times colder. I liked that.

She pulled some hair out of her face that had gotten that way because of the wind. It seemed to pick up speed. Her dress waved like a flag. "TJ, shit is crazy now. Your sister is out there. Your brothers are monsters. They got all kinds of niggas running behind them in the streets. From what I hear, they say that when you touch down, you're going to be murdered for what you did to y'all father. I'm worried about you. Oh, and Punkin says hi." She rolled her eyes and hugged me again.

I pulled her away. "Fuck you mean my little sister is out there? You mean living on her own or somethin'?" I asked feeling sick.

She shook her head. "N'all, she's selling pussy to older niggas, from what I hear. The streets say your old man turned her out because she needed to bring in an income. It's screwed up. Oh, and your mother is in the hospital. She got cancer." I wasn't even five minutes free and already I was feeling like I should have never been released. I felt like collapsing. My throat got tight, and my eyes began to water.

First my sister's news, and then my mother's. Man, I didn't know if I wanted to know about anything else. I didn't feel strong enough. When I first saw Sodi I started to contemplate on how I could have her and Miss Jackie climb into the bed with me at the same time. After all, it was my birth and release day. But after she told me this, I just felt sick. "Sodi, where are you staying now?"

"This is crazy, but I stay right across the street from Miss Jackie. I just moved there with my mother and sister two months ago. We've gotten real close. She's pretty cool."

I nodded and hugged her to my chest. "It's good to see you, baby. Soon as I figure out what's going on with my peoples you know I'ma hit this pussy, right?" I rubbed that ass again.

She snickered and nodded. "Yeah, I've kept it on lock for you."

I didn't know if I believed that, but I honestly didn't care. I was so concerned about my mother and sister that I couldn't think about anything else.

When I got into the Porsche, Miss Jackie took one look at me and mugged Sodi. "What the fuck you tell my baby?"

"I told him everything. I figured that he should know about it right away. There is no use of keeping it from him."

Miss Jackie shook her head and kissed my cheek. "It's okay, baby. I'm here for you. Before we start the day, I'ma take you over to see your mother. She knows you're coming and really wants to see you. I think it'll help you to get stronger."

I nodded. "Yeah, that sound like a plan." My mind was racing like a bunch of horses around a track.

* * *

An hour later, I walked into my mother's hospital room, just as she was sitting up. She looked pale. Her hair was stringy. There were bags under her eyes. And she had so many machines hooked up to her that it scared me nearly to death. I rushed to her side and wrapped her in my arms. Careful to not land on anyone of the cords, or IVs. "Mama, when did this happen? When did you find out?" I asked, trying my best to not break down in front of her.

She tried her best to hug me as tight as she could. But it was weak. So weak that tears came from my eyes. Her voice was strained. "I just found out a few months ago. I'ma beat this. I ain't got no other choice." She started to cough.

I pat her on the back, and Miss Jackie rushed and grabbed her juice from the tray, placed the straw to her mouth so she could sip from it. My mother drank, then leaned back against her pillows.

"What is the diagnosis?" I asked trying to keep it together. This was my mother. My heart. The love of my life. The woman that had brought me into this world. My whole life all I've ever saw was my mother struggle and be beaten into the ground by my father and brothers. Life in general. Now as I stood there watching her struggle with cancer, I just didn't understand life. "Cervical cancer. They think I had HPV for a while. I'll be undergoing chemo this week. Things will get worse, but after that they should get better. I'ma beat this. Don't worry."

I slid in the bed beside her and pulled her into my arms. Kissed her forehead, and held her. "Mama, I love you with all of my heart. Do you know that? Do you know that I would do anything for you, no matter what it is? Huh?" I was breaking down again.

I couldn't believe that my mother had cancer. My perfect angel. She exhaled loudly. "I sho wish your brothers and father felt that way. They ain't came to see me since I been in here. These people are complaining that my government insurance don't cover all of my medical bills. They been treating me real rough in here to say the least. I don't know how much more I can take." She broke into another fit of coughs. Hunched into my chest. Hawked, and grabbed a cup so she could spit into it.

Sodi grabbed it out of her hands and threw it away in the bathroom.

I rubbed my mother's back and rested my cheek against hers. "Mama, how much more do you need to get the appropriate treatment?" I asked, worried about her and wanting to blow up the hospital at the same time.

She attempted to laugh, but only wound up coughing again. "Don't you worry your little heart about that. Mama gon' be okay. What I need you to do is to find your sister and save her. She's too far gone, son. I'm worried about her. I can't begin to focus on healing not knowing if my daughter is alive and well. It's just too much. The last time I seen her she was so high that she couldn't even talk right. It broke my heart."

"Wait, Marie? My fourteen year old baby sister?" I was dumbfounded. I looked over at Sodi and she lowered her eyes.

"Yes, Marie. Find her, baby. Make sure that she's okay. You know how Chicago is. It's a heartless city. She doesn't stand a chance out there on her own." My mother grabbed my hand and kissed the back of it. "I got all of the letters you wrote me, son. They were beautiful. I am sorry that I didn't write you back, but life has been crazy out here. Your father is worse than ever."

"Mama, how much money do you need to get the best care here? Please tell me. I can't have you dying on me. I can't handle that." I hugged her closer to me.

She shrugged. "Baby, I don't even know. But it's way up there. There is no way that we can get our hands on that sum of money." She exhaled loudly. I could hear her building up to cough hard which she did.

Miss Jackie came over and rubbed her back. "Deborah, don't you worry about nothing. You just focus on getting better. Me and TJ will figure out the financial aspect of things. You hear me?" She asked looking over at me. I didn't know why she would place herself under that financial strain, but I was going to hold her to what she was saying. My mother meant the world to me. And if she was willing to help me then I would repay her with my absolute gratitude and more.

"Girl, I appreciate it. One of these days I'ma be able to pay you back. Believe that. You always have been a good friend. I mean that." She turned and opened her arms to hug Miss Jackie.

Miss Jackie hugged her back and closed her eyes. "I know it's hard Deborah, but you just gotta keep your faith in God. He'll make a way. That I know for sure."

Sodi slid beside me and placed her hand in my own. Leaned over to my ear. "TJ, can we talk out in the hallway for a minute?"

I looked over to my mother and saw that her and Miss Jackie were busy hugging and talking to one another. I figured that I could take a few minutes to holler at her. So, I nodded. "Yeah, come on." I stood up. "We gon' be in the hallway. Sodi wanna put a bug in my ear."

Miss Jackie looked irritated. "Okay, but y'all bet not dip off nowhere. We gotta make a few other stops. I also wanna hit the mall so we can get you a few outfits."

I followed Sodi out into the hallway. The first thing I noted was how busy it was. Nurses were in and out of rooms in pairs. Doctors jogged past us going this way and that. There were also other people there to visit their loved ones. I figured if she had anything important to tell me that the hallway wouldn't be the best place for us to talk. So, we wound up in the downstairs lobby, next to a big window.

She sat beside me and took my hand into hers. "Baby, I just wanted to let you know that I'm riding with you through this rough time. It sucks that your mother is sick the way that she is. If there is anything that I can do for you, please don't hesitate to let me know." She hugged me and laid her head on my shoulder.

I was confused. "Yo, that's what you called me down here for?" I asked looking down at her, a tad bit annoyed.

She sat back and looked me over. "Why? Should I have not said what I did or somethin'?"

I stood up and dusted my pants off. "N'all, I appreciate what you said, but you could have told me that upstairs. Come on. Let's go back up here before Miss Jackie get to acting some type of way. I don't feel like dealing with that right now."

Sodi stood up. "Wait, that's not it, TJ." She exhaled. "I think I might know where your sister is? Well, actually, I do know."

I frowned and pulled her close to me by her wrists. "What the fuck you mean you know where my sister at? Why you ain't been said something about that?" I was getting angry.

She took a step back and snatched her wrists from me. "Let me go. That hurt. Dang, you know you way bigger than me." She rubbed her right wrist and mugged me.

I stepped up to her again. Slid my hand along the side of her neck until I hand a hand full of her long, curly hair. Tightened my fingers in the strands and put my nose up against hers. "Sodi, I fuck with you, Ma. But my sister is my everything. You best be telling me where she is, or you and I are going to fall out real quick. Now, what's good?" I looked past her. Thankful that the lobby was empty. I was sure that somebody would have called the police on me. In that moment I didn't give a fuck. I felt like I was on the verge of seeing my baby sister again, and I needed to see her. I had been feeling sick ever since Sodi had pulled my coat about her well-being when I first got out of lock up.

She winced in pain, reaching behind her to try and free my fingers from her hair. But I wasn't letting her go. I needed answers. "Let me go, TJ. Please, baby. I'ma tell you everything that I know. Damn, Papi." I held her for a few seconds longer then released the strands of her hair. Some of them where caught between my fingers still. After I released her, she swung, and I ducked her slap. "Fool! Don't you ever do me like that. I'm not ya' mother. I'm not gon' let no nigga put his hands on me." She spat with her hair all over her head.

I felt like snapping at her comment, but I caught myself. I was behaving like my old man and that wasn't cool. "Yo, I'm sorry, baby. I ain't mean to do that to you. I'm just stressing about my sister, then my mother is upstairs all sick and shit. It's too much bad news for one day. That's all."

She took her scrunchie out of her hair, letting it sit around her wrist while she gathered all of her curls into a bundle, then she put her hair back into a ponytail that fell all the way down her back. "Now, if you would have let me finish, I would have been able to tell you why I am sure that I know where she is." She reached for my hand and led me back to the lobby's couch that we were sitting on previously. Once there, she turned toward me. "Your sister been messing with Punkin's cousin. He's this so-called pimp type dude that operates over on Howard. He has a bunch of young, high school girls that works under him selling pussy. He gets them all hopped up on heroin and pills, and they fuck like rabbits. He collects all of the profits and they basically get nothing. His name is Jax, and he moved down here from Detroit about five months ago. I asked Punkin about fifteen minutes ago if she knew if Marie was still in Jax's care? She texted me back and said she'd just seen the pair two hours ago."

I felt like I was ready to blow. "You think my sister selling pussy? At fourteen? Really, Sodi?" I felt like I was on the verge of breaking down. I couldn't imagine no shit like that. In my eyes Marie was still like three years old. I felt like I was just carrying her all around the house like when we were real little, and I'd fall trying to carry her. I still remembered when she sucked on pacifiers. Needed her pamper changed and wet the bed. To imagine her working under some Pimp was devastating to me. I just couldn't see it.

Sodi took my hand and exhaled. "TJ, I don't know what she's doing for sure, but all I can tell you is what he's known for. She been in his care for over three months. Only God knows what he's made her do. We can only try our best to get to her as soon as possible."

I sat there dumbfounded. Dropped my head between my legs and tried my best to not imagine my sister being misled like that. I didn't know how I would react if I ran into this Jax nigga. I was already having some murderous thoughts going through my brain. Then, every time I thought about how my father and brothers had dropped the ball with the women in our family it made me begin to hate them more and more. I stood up and pulled Sodi to her feet. "Come on. Let's get back up here so I can say goodbye to my mother, then you about to show me where this nigga be at. I ain't laying my head on my pillow until I talk to my sister. That's my word."

Chapter 9

Sodi made her way to Miss Jackie's black on black Mercedes Benz, got in and slammed the door. I could see her through the glass pulling her seatbelt around her as I stepped out onto the porch, getting ready to jump into her whip so I could go and find my sister. It was still my first day out, about five o'clock at night. The sun was shining bright. There was a gentle breeze that made the approaching night appear almost comfortable. Had my head not been so screwed up I would have been able to enjoy it on some level.

Before I could step down the first step, Miss Jackie grabbed my right arm roughly and pulled me back into her home. "Wait a minute, TJ. I need to speak some sense into your brain before you go over there and get yourself into trouble." As she said this, her husband walked out of the house and kissed her on the cheek and kept right on his merry way as if he didn't want to get involved. I didn't know what was going on with them at this point, and I didn't care. My mind was focused on my sister, Marie. So, when she pulled me back into her home, I got irritated because I knew that time was ticking. She closed the door behind us and stood in front of me.

"Look, Miss Jackie, I hear everything you've already said. I ain't going over here to get in no trouble. I just want to talk to my sister. Try to see if I can talk some sense into her. That's all. You ain't got nothin' to worry about."

She looked into my eyes for a few moments, then surrendered. "Okay, baby, just be careful. I don't want anything to happen to you. You're my little heart. Do you know that?" She stepped forward and kissed me on the lips. Held the back of my head until we were tonguing each other down.

My hands gripped that ripe ass with reckless abandon. When our lips popped apart we were both breathing hard.

"Baby, when you get back here tonight, we're going to finish this."

I wiped my lips and nodded, then thought about it. "How we gon' do that with yo' husband here?" I opened the door, preparing to step back outside.

She scoffed. "Don't even worry about him. He gon' have his ass full with his lil' boyfriend. Me and that man ain't slept together since I found out that he been sleeping with men. I'll be damned if he give me AIDs. No thank you. Besides, he's too old for me." She smiled and stepped up, kissing me again.

I slightly closed the door back so Sodi couldn't see what we were on. I didn't feel like arguing with her either. "Aight then, that sound like a plan. I'll see you a lil' later." I stepped out of the door and jogged down the stairs. Got into the car and closed the door. "Look, when we get around this block, you gon' jump behind this steering wheel. You got your L's don't you?" I asked her.

"You fucking that old bitch, TJ?" She said this without looking over at me. Simply looked out of the big windshield.

"Yo, right now ain't the time to go through all of that shit, Sodi. Like I said, when we get around this corner, I'ma have you drive because I ain't trying to have these Chicago Twelves fucking with me. So, you gon' jump behind the wheel and rollout to the Northside; do you hear me?"

She looked over at me and frowned. "Yeah, nigga. I heard you. Now answer the fucking question. Are you fucking that old bitch? Be a man and tell me what's good?" She sat up in her seat. Now she was mugging me with hatred in her eyes.

I started up the car and a track by Ella Mae came out of the speakers. Threw the car in drive and pulled from in front of the house. I drove about two blocks in silence. Then, I pulled over and got out of the car. By the time I made it back to her passenger's side she was still sitting there as if she were protesting. I opened her passenger's door and nudged her ass. "Get yo' ass over there behind the wheel and quit acting so fuckin' stubborn. Damn."

She sat still for a second them climbed across the console. "Nigga, I'll sit here but I ain't pulling off until you tell me what's good. Are you fucking this bitch or not?"

I sat in the passenger's seat and slammed the door. "Yeah. I am. Now what? Last time I checked you ain't dropping no bread on me. You ain't rolling no Benz, and you sho wasn't able to get inside of the prison and do the shit that she was able to do. So, hell yeah, we done fucked a few times. I'm pretty sure you done gave some nigga the pussy while I was on lock." I don't know why I was being so bogus toward her. Maybe it was because I was irritated in general at finding out all that I had. That was coupled with the fact that I had been so excited to get out of prison that I had not slept in two days. So, I was a bit groggy. I honestly liked Sodi. Not on no super serious shit, but I cared about her feelings. I just wasn't in the mood.

She nodded. "Okay. That's what's up. At least now I know, and they say knowing is half the battle." She pulled off and drove the rest of the way in silence. Since she didn't have nothing else to say, I didn't either. As far as I was concerned, at the end of the day, she wasn't nothing but a shot of pussy. She ain't have her own money like Miss Jackie. She ain't have no whips, cribs, businesses, nothing. Just a good mouthpiece on her shoulders that I was looking forward to trying out. And a wet shot between her legs that I needed to bust open the right way. I had so much other things on my mind, I just couldn't cater to her emotional needs. And even though it picked at me a little bit, I got over it, quick.

* * *

As luck would have it, when we pulled onto the block of Howard, my sister was just walking out of a Popeye's restaurant with a bag of food. Some grown ass, fat nigga had his arm around her shoulder all possessive like. He looked like he had to be in his late thirties. My sister wore a pair of shorts that were so small that the back halves of her ass cheeks were hanging out of them. Her thighs were on display as well. She also had on a belly shirt that stopped just below the swells of her breasts. The bottom portion of the mounds were visible. She looked like she'd put on ten pounds in all the wrong places which were her backside, thighs and chest. She looked like a grown woman, but I knew better.

My heart started pounding so bad that I felt like I was about to pass out. "Yo, stop the car. That's my baby sister right there." I ordered Sodi with my door already opening. Sodi slammed on the brakes, and I jumped out of the Benz and jogged across the street toward the pair. "Marie! Marie! What the fuck you doing out here!" I said running up on them.

Jax pulled an all-black Glock out of his waistband and aimed it at me. "Nigga, who the fuck is you?"

I grabbed my sister by the wrist and pulled her away from him. "Bitch ass nigga, if you gon' shoot, you better kill me. That's my word." I mugged him with hatred, wishing I was packing because if I had been I would have smoked him right there with no hesitation.

Marie fell into my embrace with her eyes so low that all I could make out was her pupils. "TJ? Big bruh, is that you?"

Jax looked both ways and snatched the bag of food out of Marie's hands. "Nigga, if you want some of this pussy it's gon' cost you two hundred. If not, let my bitch go, or I'm about to slump you right here in front of everybody."

I pulled Marie behind me. "Nigga, what? Do it then. Pull the trigger you bitch ass nigga. What you waiting on?"

Sodi came running across the street with her cellphone to her ear. "Wait, Jax, that's his little sister. That's his little sister. She only fourteen!" She yelled.

Jax's eyes got big. He put the pistol back on his waist and pulled his shirt over it. "Aw, see I ain't know all of that. That's some shit you gotta lead with." He looked both ways again. There was a bunch of people looking at us from in front of their buildings. The Popeye's was located right on the corner of Howard. An alley separated where the houses began so people were able to see us clearly. Jax extended his hand. "I think me and you need to talk, homie." He smiled.

"Talk?" I smacked his hand from in front of me so hard that it turned him sideways. "Bitch ass nigga, you lucky I ain't got that cannon on me, 'cause if I did, my word, I'd smoke you like some hot links." I put my arm around my sister and walked off on his ass, heated. So heated that my vision was blurry.

"It's all good, bruh, just bring her back in one piece. If you don't, she gon' wind up making her way back to me anyway." He sucked his teeth and walked off. Halfway down the block a group of young girls ran over to comfort him. It was sickening.

Fifteen minutes later me and Marie sat in the backseat of Miss Jackie's car while it was parked at the lakefront. Sodi had chosen to give us a little privacy. I kissed my sister on the forehead and allowed for her to lay on my chest.

"TJ, as soon as you left, Daddy really started in on me. It went from him ordering mama to let me sleep with him once a week, to every single day. If ever he came home and I wasn't already in the bed waiting on him, he would beat mama senseless. He never laid a hand on me that way, just every other." She shook her head and exhaled. Her breath smelled like Double Mint gum. Me and my sister had always been sticklers about fresh breath and good hygiene.

"And when did Deion bitch ass start going in on you?" I asked. I was so mad that I felt like I was boiling. I couldn't believe that they would molest my sister the way that they had. It was hard for me to digest, so I could only imagine how it was truly effecting her.

She was silent for a second. "Deion only did it to me twice, but he made me suck his stuff like five times. JD was more of a problem than him. I don't know how many times he forced himself on me. I just know that it's too many times to count." She rose her head from my chest. "Why do you think they did me like that, TJ? What have I ever done to either of them?" She broke into a fit of tears, holding me as tight as she could.

I pressed my lips against her forehead and just held them there. Eyes misty in disbelief. I couldn't understand how I had come from such a terrible family of men. I couldn't believe how they talked to my mother, beat her, and allowed for her to undergo so much pain and agony at the hands of our father. Then when it came to our precious little sister, how they could do the things that they had done to her. I felt beyond sick. I didn't know what to say to her. What possibly could I have?

"Then, I guess once Daddy got sick of me, he just put me out. He said that I was dead weight. That since I didn't bring in any income that I was worthless to him. That's when I hit the streets and ran into Jax. One of my homegirls from school put me in with him, and he gave me a place to stay, amongst other things." She shook her head and held me tighter once again.

"Well, you ain't about to work for that nigga no more. I'm home now and I'ma take care of you like I'm supposed to. I ain't gon' let nobody hurt you. You hear me?"

She sat up and removed some hair from her forehead. Placed it behind her right earlobe. "There's one more thing. Look." She held out her right arm. Being this close I could smell her deodorant mixed with a slight hint of sweat. She rubbed over the track marks along her inner forearm. "I'm hooked, big bruh. Like I need it all the time. In fact, I'm starting to feel sick right now. You don't want these problems. I'm a lost cause. I assure you of that." She sniffled and wiped away her tears.

I was so devastated that all I could do was pull her to my chest and wrap my arms around her small frame. "I love you, Marie, and I'ma help you beat that addiction, sis. I promise."

She shook her head again. "No, see, that's the thing. I don't want any help, TJ. I'm good. Ever since I been getting high I been free. Nothing in the world can hurt me as long as I stay up in the clouds. When I'm up there, nothing that Daddy did to me hurts. Nothing that Deion and JD did to me hurts, and do you know that they've had me at the same time before?" She started to cry harder. "I just want to be free from all of this. It's too much. I can't handle it. Please don't take me away."

"Marie, I'm not about to let you go down the drain like this, lil' sis. You're only fourteen. You have so much life ahead of you. We can still make it out of these slums together. You're my heart. It's always been you and I, even before you could barely walk. I would be less than a man to give up on you right now while you're at your lowest point. It's my job to protect you. You're my angel, sis. I love you with all of me." Now tears were running down my cheeks. Nothing ever got me more emotional than my mother and sister. I think it was because I knew that neither of them ever really had a fair chance in life. Since the beginning my sister had been against the odds. The only girl in a house full of men. Three out of the four men in our household looked at her as prey, and I was the only one that looked down to my sister as one that I should protect and love with all of myself. Placing her needs above and before my own.

She sniffled and laid her face against mine. "I just hate myself, TJ. I feel filthy all of the time. Every time I close my eyes, it's like I can replay what they've done to me. It's all I see. The only thing that numbs the pain is this heroin. I need it just to get by. I am not strong enough to get by without it." She shivered. "I'm seriously getting sick as we speak. Jax hasn't given me anything because I had to turn a trick first. But it's time. Please, let's go get some. I'll die if we don't."

I held her in my arms, feeling her shake as if she were freezing. I didn't want to let her go. Didn't want to release her because I feared what had to take place next. I was so sick over all that I'd found out. Broken because of the things my sister had to endure without me being there to protect her. I felt like I'd dropped the ball. Like I should have never did what I did to our father because, had I not, I would have been able to protect her from the monsters that were in our home.

That night, I sat across from my sister as she got her works ready in Miss Jackie's guest bedroom. I watched her cook her dope before drawing it up into her syringe. She tied a rope around her left arm before injecting herself full of heroin that I'd bought for her. Watching my fourteen-year-old sister shoot the poison in her arm caused me to fall into my lowest state of depression. I watched the sweat slide down the side of her face. Her eyes rolled into the back of her head before she dislodged the syringe and slumped to her bottom on the carpet. The light from the lamp illuminating her face.

She smacked her lips and smiled. "I just want to be happy, TJ. I don't want to feel the pain anymore. Please hold me. I need you so bad. Just hold me." She opened her arms wide and reached out for me.

I slid on the floor and into her arms. Hugging her. Kissing her forehead. "It's okay, baby sis. I got you. I'ma hold you down no matter what you're going through. We're in this thing together. Until the end. Right?"

She nodded and smiled. "Until the end."

Before the night was out, my sister would shoot up two more times before she passed out against me. We fell asleep together, hugged up on the floor. When I woke up the next morning she was gone.

Chapter 10

I spent the next two weeks looking for my sister everywhere. No matter where I checked or whoever I asked, everyone acted as if they didn't know where she was, and after a while it started to break me down even more. It got to the point that after I'd spend ten hours a day rolling Miss Jackie's Benz looking for her, and I came up unsuccessful, I'd come back and lock myself in Miss Jackie's guestroom and sit in the dark. My sister had left her shirt there, and I'd hold it tight in my fist, close to my face to smell her scent. I missed her so bad that it was starting to fuck with my mental. I was worried and didn't know what to do.

One Sunday morning, Miss Jackie took a butter knife and picked her way into the room by jimmying the lock. Flipped on the light, walked past the bed and flipped open the curtains. "Boy, get yo' ass up. Your friend Juelz is parked outside, waking my neighbors up with that loud ass truck of his. I need you to go out there and see what he want." She leaned over and kissed my lips. "Oh, and good morning." She walked out of the room with her big booty jiggling in her all white lace boy shorts.

I had my eyes pinned on that ass. I felt like crap because I still hadn't been able to fuck her since I'd been released from prison. I had too much shit on my mind to be able to go there mentally, but my nature was calling. I knew it wouldn't be long before I was waxing that ass like I was supposed to. I honestly needed that relief just as bad as she did. "Miss Jackie, come here real quick." I called out to her just as she walked past the threshold of the bedroom and into the hallway.

She stopped in her tracks and turned around. "Yeah, baby? What's the matter?" She wore a tight pink tank top that showed off her puffy nipple imprints. There were nice shots of her side boob too. She was an attractive older woman.

I needed her healing. I grabbed her by her hand and pulled her into the bed on top of me. Ran my hands over her lower back, then cupped her ass cheeks. Pulled the material all the way into her ass crack so that whole chocolate ass was on display. It looked so good with a few stretch marks across each cheek.

"Um, baby. What's on your mind?" She asked, licking my lips.

My dick was super hard because I had just woken up. I knew she could feel it. I needed a quickie. Something to take my mind off of my sister if only for a few moments. "Pull these to the side." I said, yanking her material to the right side of her pussy from the back. "Now sit on your son, mama. I just need you real quick before I greet this day." I squeezed her booty, then slid my fingers into her crack again. Peeling her pussy lips wise open. They felt hot and steamy.

She licked my neck. "Okay, baby, but my husband is upstairs. What if he catch us?" She moaned, grabbed my dick out of my boxers and lined me up. Then she pushed back on my helmet and swallowed me whole. Sank down until she was sitting on my balls. Her hands squeezed my chest, then she was riding me fast. Her tight pussy was sucking at me like a Hoover vacuum cleaner. "Fuck." She gasped with her head thrown back.

I held that big booty, squeezing it. Holding on to it while she rode me like a pro. It felt so good. Her juices were already creaming out of her. We were sopping wet between our sexes in no time. She bounced up and down, causing the headboard to slam into the wall of the guest room. "Aw. Miss Jackie. Damn. This pussy so. It's so. Damn." I couldn't even think straight.

She started popping her back and riding me faster. "You're my baby. My baby. Uh. Fuck, TJ. Uh. I love you so much. This my dick. Mine. Uh, fuck. Son." She sucked my neck hard. Her hips rotated in a circular motion faster and faster.

I started to make little sounds that embarrassed me. But when the pussy was good, it'll make a nigga do that on a regular. I squeezed my eyes together, moaned out loud, and opened them, just in time to see her husband standing in the doorway looking at us with a frown on his face. I grabbed Miss Jackie's hips and forced her to ride me faster. "Ma, yo' nigga looking at us. Uh. He looking, Ma."

She slowed her jockeying, looked over her shoulder, and made eye contact with him. "What do you want?" She shouted, riding me slowly.

I looked down and saw how my dick went in and out of her bald pussy. Opening it wide before it swallowed me, then my piece would appear all shiny. It was hot. She turned all the way around and placed her back to my face. Slid me back into her and rode me reverse cowgirl while her husband watched us as quiet as a church mouse. I sat up and pulled her titties out of her shirt. Playing with them while she rode me.

"How could you, Jackie?" He asked stepping closer to the bed.

She sped up her pace. Arched her back and rode me like a savage. I was whimpering like crazy. That big ass was shaking along with her thighs. When she leaned all the way forward and placed her palms on the bed she started twerking in my lap. It was too much. I came all in her womb. And because she felt me shooting her tunnel up, she squeezed her eyes tight; rode me faster until she came, screaming at the top of her lungs. Her husband ran out of the room, just as the doorbell started to ring over and over again.

Miss Jackie hopped off of me and sucked her juices off of my pipe. "Baby, go do your thing, but be careful out there. You can take the Benz, and I left a hundred-dollar bill on your dresser. I gotta go in here and smooth this shit out with him." She rolled her eyes.

* * *

93

Juelz handed me a blunt rolled so fat that it looked like a mini brown newspaper. I set fire to it as he pulled onto the highway. "Yeah, bruh, like I said, I ain't been fucking around in Chicago. I been getting it with my cousins out in Brooklyn. It's crazy cash out there. It's like a whole other world. How they get down out there it make us Chicago niggas seem like bums. We need to fly out there so I can get you acquainted with the fellas. Straight up."

I nodded, but my mind was somewhere else. "Bruh, I wanna kill my old man and my brothers. I'm talking like tonight, if at all possible." I took four tokes of the blunt and held the smoke, passed it to him, and grabbed the bottle of Pepsi I'd been sippin' on. I had made my mind up. I wasn't gon' be able to get a clear head until I was able to wet them niggas up. I couldn't allow for them to be breathing after what they'd did to my sister.

Juelz inhaled the smoke sharply and blew it toward the cracked window of his Lexus truck. "Somethin' you wanna tell me?" He asked, looking me over.

"Shortly after I got knocked, all of them niggas started going in on my sister, bruh. Doing all types of real foul shit to her. Messed her up so bad that she fucking with that heroin real tough, hoeing, and now I can't find her. If it wasn't for them bitch niggas, none of that would have happened. So, I wanna send them chumps on they way. That's just that." He handed me back the blunt and I took it.

He shook his head. "That's foul, bruh. It's a reason I never liked yo' peoples though. Them niggas just rub me the wrong way. But you sure you wanna stank 'em. I mean they still are your blood. Once we smoke they ass, they gone. My word. It ain't gon' mean shit to me. I promise you. But can you live with the aftermath?"

The way I was feeling, I was sure that I could. Every time I imagined one of them niggas crawling on top of my sister and holding her down while they took advantage of her, it vexed me and made me want to kill something. "Yo, I live with it. I need to take these niggas off of the map. Point blank."

Juelz got into the fast lane, then flipped the truck on cruise control. Reached between his legs and handed me a Mach .11. "Here, bruh. This got thirty-two shots in it. I know where that nigga JD serving packs at right now. He fuck with this lil' red bone bitch over on Jarvis out north. I got a bitch in the building; she'll let us in. If you wanna smoke this nigga then we can take care of his ass tonight. What's good?"

My heart started beating fast as hell as I looked the Mach over in my hands. It was oh so pretty. The clip stuck out of the bottom of it like a Pez dispenser. "I say we rollout, and I'ma make this bitch spit for my lil' sister. Let God forgive this nigga because I can't." I set the Mach on my lap, imagining me blowing out my little brother's brains. I ain't gon' lie and say that I wasn't scared because I was terrified.

I mean, that was still my flesh and blood. I had never killed anybody before, and for the first person to be my own brother? Man, I was freakin' out of my mind. But I had to flex like it wasn't no big deal in front of Juelz. That nigga was used to knocking heads off. Had what happened to my sister happened to anybody that he cared about, he would have murdered all of the culprits with no hesitation. Blood or not. I needed to get into his murderous mind state. It was going to take some time. But the more I imagined them hurting my sister, the angrier I got, and the thought of murdering something became less of a problem.

Juelz nodded. "Yo, before we hit up that nigga, I want you to go on a run with me over to Gary, Indiana." He laid his seat back and turned up *Tha Carter* CD. Lil' Wayne banged out of the speakers.

I nodded my head to it. In my opinion, there was nobody colder than Wayne when it came to spitting that heat. "What's in Gary?" I asked, puffing on the blunt.

He looked over at me and smiled. "I gotta hit these two bosses up. The pay is twenty bands for each one. If you come along with me, I'll give you half. And if you handle yo' business on this move, then I'll put you up on another one that pays double what we'll get from this one." He took the blunt back and started to puff. He dumped the ashes in the ashtray.

I was so high that my ears were ringing. My eyes werc low as hell, and I was high as the roof on top of a house. "Yo, so what, you clapping niggas for bread now?"

He snickered. "I can't sit in no trap all day and catch money the slow way. And that robbing shit is cool, but I always wind up clapping a nigga anyway, so I figured why not cut out all of the middle shit and go right for the gusto. I get no less than twenty for a body. I'm in and out of cities, do my thing, and keep it moving. Get my scratch and cop shit like this truck I'm driving. In case you haven't figured it out, you're a bum, nigga. You ain't got shit. You're trash right now. You ain't no kid no more. You're a man. And now that you are a man, let me be the first to tell you that nobody gives a fuck about you unless you got that green. This world will piss on a broke nigga. So, I ain't going. I'm tryna put you on to something for ya self." He steered into the middle lane, then back to the far left one. Beside us, the El train screeched past on its tracks. It was packed with a bunch of commuters.

"Yo, why you ain't write me when I was down, bruh?" I don't know where that question came from. I guess the thought of me busting a major out of town move with a nigga that had neglected to stand by my side while I was on lock somewhat spooked me. It wasn't that I didn't trust my nigga. I just felt real funny around him now.

"Yo, bitches write letters, man. Not niggas. Every time I was in town, I made sure I hit ya' sister with a few bands. Her and Sodi. That paper should have made its way back to you. I ain't writing no nigga in jail, and I wouldn't expect a nigga to write me either. That's all I'ma say. On top of that, I was locked for eight months of the time that you was. So, shit ain't been peachy for me either. Until recently." He stubbed the blunt out. "So, you rolling with me or what?"

There was no way that I could see myself passing up twenty bands. My mother needed help with her doctor bills, and real soon I was gon' have to find a place of my own. Even though Miss Jackie had some good ass pussy, I still needed my own independence so I could take my sister in when I found her. "Give me the gist. What we gotta do?" I turned down the radio so I could hear him out.

"It's real simple. We got two marks. I got their addresses, and places they are going to be. We track them down, put a couple slugs in their faces and keep it moving. Neither one of the licks should take more than a few minutes as long as we do it right. I'm like fifteen in, and shit been going real smooth so far. Nah'mean?" He turned on his blinkers and switched lanes, then stepped on the gas. "I'm hungry as a bitch. Yo, at this next exit, I'ma pull off and get a box of chicken. You hungry?" He turned to look at me, then back to the road.

My stomach growled. Ever since my lil' sister had been missing in action I'd been passing up meals left and right. Me and Miss Jackie often got into arguments about this. She said that I was losing weight and she didn't like it. In my opinion I was still real muscular. I may have lost about five pounds, but it didn't hurt me none. But I was starving, especially after taking her ass down. "That sound good to me, bruh, long as you paying for it." I figured if he was fifteen jobs in at a minimum of twenty gees a piece that he was way up. A box of chicken wasn't gon' hurt his pockets, but it would hurt mine.

He laughed and looked over at me. "Nigga, you funny. But I got you though. And don't trip, I'm gon' get you right. I ain't about to be seeing chips and you're hurting. What the fuck type of nigga would that make me?" He navigated the whip so that we wound up in the far-right lane, then he got off on Cottage Grove.

The whole time I was trying to wrap my head around killing niggas for cash. I didn't know if I had that in me or not. I mean it was real easy to say that you were a killer until it was time to do it. That took heart. As much as I hated my brothers, I swore up and down that I could kill one of them easily, but when the time came I really wondered if I would have been able to. After I'd pistol whipped my Pops, I had nightmares and felt some type of way, so I was nervous and didn't know if I had that killer shit in me yet.

Juelz pulled off of the Exit ramp, drove a few blocks and we wound up in the drive thru of KFC with two cars ahead of us, waiting to place their orders. That's when a money green Lexus pulled up alongside of Juelz's truck, and I saw Punkin trying to flag us down. She was hanging halfway out of the window with her arms wagging crazily.

Juelz had managed to pull a .40 Caliber from out of the seat. It had a beam attached to the top of it. He mugged her car, and when he saw that it was her, he took a deep breath and sat back in his seat. "Yo, I almost blasted that bitch. Fuck. Get out and see what she want. I'll just walk in and order the food."

I nodded and stepped out of the car after sliding the Mach back under my seat.

Punkin jumped out of her whip, and ran to me, jumped into my arms and wrapped her thick legs around me along with her arms. "Damn, TJ. I can't believe you're out. You're finally out. I been trying to get into contact with you ever since you got popped off almost two years ago. What's good?"

She smelled so good. I sat her back down onto her feet and looked her over. She had on a nice red, white, and gray Moschino fit, with the matching Jordan's. Her hair was freshly whipped. She had cut her hair shoulder-length and flipped into tight curls. She looked slimmer in the face, but thicker in the body. She looked like a woman, and I was taken aback. Her lips had gotten juicier, and for me that was a game changer.

I frowned a bit. "Why you ain't just get my info from Sodi, or from Miss Jackie? Both of them knew where I was." I wasn't buying her bullshit. Even though she was looking good as hell, I had to keep in mind that she'd neglected me once I'd gotten locked up, even after I'd whooped that nigga Blue for trying to force himself upon her.

She shook her head. "N'all, don't do that. Every time I tried to ask Miss Jackie about you, that bitch told me not to worry about you. That you were good. And Sodi said that she didn't know your address. That she was putting her letters in with Miss Jackie. So, I gave her three letters to send to you along with hers and Miss Jackie's, but she said that Miss Jackie snapped and cut her off from mailing you as well. I don't know. But I swear to you, I tried." She got giddy again. "I can't believe you're home. You gotta come chill with me. I got my own place over on Sheraton. It's nice. A two-bedroom, one bath, fireplace, balcony. It's cool for a first crib. Please tell me that you can come and mess with me?"

Juelz came out of KFC with a big bag of food. Walked over to us and nodded at Punkin. "What's good, Shorty? I see you done got thick as hell." He sucked some pop through the straw of his drink, looking down at her.

Punkin rolled her eyes. "Hey, Juelz. You talk to yo' baby mama lately?" She rolled her eyes again, then looked back to me. "Anyway, so you gon' come chill with me?"

I looked her up and down and knew for a fact that I wasn't about to pass that ass up. Not only that, but I had always had a thing for Punkin growing up. Now that she was a woman, I wanted to explore it. I handed her my phone. "Put yo' info in there, and I'ma get at you as soon as I get back in town."

She took it and started to add her stuff to it. "Dang, when you supposed to be back?"

Juelz laughed. "Damn, Shorty, you ain't seen my nigga in damn near two years and you already sweating him.

That's funny. I should turn his ass out to these Spanish bitches I got lined up for tomorrow night. I guarantee he won't remember yo' ass if I do that." He snickered again. Punkin stepped to the side of me so she could stand a few feet closer to him. "Why don't you mind yo' fuckin business, nigga. Don't worry about how I'm sweating him. You should be worrying about the ten baby mamas you got running around Chicago with no support from yo' trifling ass. Ugh." She turned to me. "When are you getting back, TJ? I'm tryna fuck with you." She stepped so close to me that I couldn't help but to wrap my arms around her waist, and slide my hands down to her ass, cuffing them cheeks. She moved out of my embrace and blushed, and that made me feel some type of way. Punkin had always been a real proper, low key female.

"We should be back first thing in the morning. I'ma hit you up and see what it do then. Oh, but before I forget. What's this I hear about my sister supposed to be selling pussy for your cousin, Jax? What you know about that?"

She shrugged. "I don't mess with him like that. I ran into your sister twice since you been gone. And one of those times I saw her with him, but I didn't think nothing of it. If you're thinking I hooked them up, then that wasn't the case. I would never disrespect you like that. Especially after what you did for me back in the day."

"Can we please go? This sentimental ass moment is making me sick to my stomach. Bruh, she trying to give you some pussy. It's long overdue. Let's head out here and get back so you can smash her thick ass. That's gon' be that. Damn."

"Shut up, Juelz. Dang, ain't nobody said nothing about screwing. That's all you think about. Probably why you got so many kids!" Punkin hollered and he walked off on her and got back into the truck.

"Anyway, I'ma be at you as soon as I can. If you can find your cousin for me, that'll really help me right now. My sister been missing for a minute, and I'm worried about her. Come here."

She walked into my arms and I hugged her again. The scent of her perfume was intoxicating. "I got you, TJ. I'll start trying to locate him as soon as I get back in my car. I'm sorry you gotta go through that. Please hit me up as soon as you can. I'll be waiting on you."

Chapter 11

Juelz handed me a black ski mask that he had tucked into the driver's seat. "Look, I fuck with this white bitch that's gon' let us into the side door. She already know what's good. We gon' go in there, pop her husband and his brother, and be out. After we hit they ass up, you come on back out to the truck and I'ma handle her because she gotta go, too. Once we pull this over, we gon' head to the southside, and we gotta hit two more people. You got that?" He placed his ski mask on the top of his head and prepared to roll it down.

"Wait, nigga. You made it seem like we was only hitting a couple people. Now you saying five. Fuck is you on?" I asked mugging his nutty ass. I should have known that it was more to it than he'd let on. There always was whenever I dealt with Juelz. I could never take his ass at face value. It was the story of our friendship.

"It's fifty gees in it for you. Fifty. I might've lied about the body count, but I also lied about the bread you was gon' make. You'll gross thirty gees more. Now, tell me that ain't worth it." He pulled the mask all the way down and looked out of the car. We were parked on a residential street full of houses that looked expensive. All of the lawns were mown in the neighborhood from as far as I could see. And the cars and trucks that were parked in driveways looked like the newer models for the brands.

"Bruh, are we slumping white folks?"

He handed me a pair of leather gloves. "I don't know why that surprise you. What? You scared to kill a Yankee or somethin'?" He snickered. "Not many niggas are even worth twenty gees. Ain't nobody gon' pay that shit for their murder unless their deep in the game like the two we smoking after these three. Now come on." He opened his truck door and there was a constant dinging from the interior.

I threw on the gloves and placed the .40 Caliber into my waistband and followed behind him as he walked down the quiet, dark block.

A few of the houses had their blinds raised and I could see people sitting in their living room watching television. It had to be about ten o'clock. The crickets were chirping, and the mosquitoes were out already. Juelz walked swiftly until we came to the middle of the block. Once there, he hopped the fence and looked both ways. Waved me to do the same, which I did. After we hopped the fence, I followed him to the back of the two-story brick house where he kneeled and pulled out his phone.

"Yo, I'm calling this bitch. Be ready to go."

I placed my back against the house and tried to stop my heart from beating so loud in my chest. Once again, I had placed myself in an impossible situation. I wanted with every fiber of my being to just walk back to the truck and tell him I was good. Fuck the money. I would find another way to help my mother get right. I couldn't take a person's life for nothing. I didn't even know if I could take a person's life if they did something serious to me like my father and brothers had. I was so confused and scared to say the least. I was having second, third, and fourth thoughts about everything. Maybe I wasn't cut out for this. That nigga Juelz was already nuts. I had common sense.

We waited for two minutes, and then the side door came open. A white girl with long red hair stepped out of the door, and shielding her eyes, looking for Juelz I guessed because there was no sun out. She dared to walk toward the back of the house when he sprang out at her.

She yelped and he wound up behind her with his hand over her mouth. "Shh, be quiet. It's good. Tell me where everybody is." He slowly took his hand away from her mouth but remained behind her.

She kept her voice low. "My husband just got in the shower. His brother is drunk off his ass, laying on the living room couch watching the Bear and Packer game. My daughter is upstairs sleeping. That's all the people in the house."

"Are you sure?" He whispered with his face against hers. She nodded. "I'm sure. Remember it has to look like a break in so really trash the place. You already know the combination to the safe. Just make sure I get half of the money and jewelry back. Cool?"

This part through me for a loop. He didn't tell me nothing about a safe, money, or jewelry. Juelz look back at me. "That's a good girl. Now be cool. This has to happen." He tightened his arm around her neck and started to choke her out from the back with all of his might. I could hear him grunting. She gagged and slapped at his arm. He pulled her to the back of the house where it was pitch dark and continued to choke her. "Die bitch. Die." He fell to the ground with her and finished her off. Then, he popped up and kicked her to the side of the gate. "Alright. Let's go, bruh. You heard her. One in the bathroom and one is in the living room watching the game. Which one do you want?" He kicked her again to make sure that she was well out of view.

My head was spinning like crazy. I couldn't believe that all of this shit was actually happening. "I guess I'll take dude in the shower. Catch him off guard." I imagined what I was about to do and felt like I had to shit. I was farting and everything. I figured it would be easier to hit dude in the shower because I could clap him through the shower curtain and keep it moving.

"Alright, that sound good. Let's go. I'ma fuck dude over on the couch right away. Fuck, I almost forgot. Let me see that Forty." He handed me his, with a silencer attached to it. Took the one I had and screwed a silencer into its barrel. Then we were at the side door, with Juelz leading the way. He twisted the knob, and pushed it in.

A big ass Golden Retriever ran down the steps and straight toward us. Juelz jumped backward into me and aimed his gun at the dog. But the dog ran past us and into the back yard, chasing its tail, then hopping up and down as if it could not believe it was outside.

I nudged him forward with my heart in my mouth. "Damn, nigga. I ain't know what you was jumping back for." I looked over at the dog. He ran out of view, barking twice, then was quiet.

We crept up the side stairs and into the first floor landing of the house. I could hear the television blasting the football game. A male's voice cursing at the television. Yelling that the referee who had made a bad call. Juelz placed his gloved finger to his lips and waved me to follow him. He knelt just a tad and sped up the pace of his strides. We entered into a kitchen, and then a short hallway that had white carpet along it. I kept my back sliding along the wall. I still could barely breathe. I was starting to panic, but it was too late to turn back now. I was all in. Had to be. Juelz had already slumped a bitch in my face. If I backed out now I was sure that he would have become suspicious. I know I would have.

When we came out of the hallway, I could see the heavy-set white man clear as day now. He sat straight up on the couch with a box of pizza opened in front of him, and about ten beers on the top of the table next to a bowl of nachos. He was balding at the top of his head and had a Bear's jersey on that appeared to be too small for him. The bottom half of his belly hung out of it. Hairy and nasty looking.

Juelz held me back, stopped abruptly, and held up his hand to me. "Watch this shit." He rushed over and ran up on the man, shooting. His gun jumping in his hand with fire spitting from the barrel. Shells popped into the air. His bullets slamming into the man's face back to back, before the man slumped over and fell to the floor in a bloody mess.

I stood back with my eyes bucked, disbelieving. This had been the first time I'd ever seen anybody killed up close and personal, and it blew my mind. There was a heavy scent of gunpowder in the air. I swallowed and clutched my gun tighter in my hand.

Juelz pointed upstairs. "Come on, I hear the shower still going. It's your turn now." He bent down and picked his shells off of the floor, putting them into his right front pocket.

I made my way up the stairs with my gun leading the way as if I was a policeman or something. The stairs were also carpeted. The dog began to bark at the side door downstairs. I feared that his barking would cause the neighbors to become suspicious. I wanted to handle this business and get out of there. I was sweating all down my back and under my mask. My throat was dry, and my knees were trying to knock into each other. It was crazy. When I made it to the top of the stairs I could hear the shower water loud and clear.

I followed the sound until I was standing outside the bathroom door, shaking as if I was freezing cold, preparing to take an innocent man's life all in the name of money. I placed my gloved hand on the knob and got ready to turn it when I caught movement from the corner of my right eye. I snapped my head in its direction. There at the end of the hall, inside of the master bedroom, was our last mark. He stood with his back toward us with a towel around his waist, bouncing a baby girl up and down in his arms.

Juelz slapped me on the back. "Go smoke his ass, bruh, and let's get out of here," he ordered.

I nodded and slid along the wall as fast as I could. My knees were shaking. When I got about ten feet away, I took a deep breath and rushed into the room with my gun brandished. The man turned around with his eyes wide.

"Put the baby down now, muthafucka!" I knew I had to knock his head off, but I didn't want to risk killing a little kid. That shit wasn't in me. "Do it now!"

He backed all the way up, holding the back of the baby's head. "Please, don't do this. If it's money you want, there fifty grand in my safe, and some jewelry. Please don't hurt us." He begged.

"Man, shoot his bitch ass, bruh. Kill him. This ain't no negotiation mission. Hurry the fuck up." Juelz snapped.

I shook my gun in his face. "Put the baby down. Do it or I'ma kill you and that kid." I lied. I didn't give a fuck what went down, I wasn't about to air at this white dude as long as he was holding that baby. I would have never been able to live with myself if I killed a kid. Fuck what Juelz was talking about. I couldn't do it.

"Please. I'll do anything. Just don't do this to us. Please." The white man begged.

"Blood, smoke his bitch ass. Do it. Do it." Juelz ordered. He looked back from them, to me, and shook his head. "Fuck it." Stepped forward and started to bust his gun back to back just as he had downstairs. The first two bullets knocked big chunks of the man's head off. It splattered across the walls. He fell to his knees and dropped the baby. The baby began to scream at the top of her lungs. Juelz stepped over it and aimed his gun. Pulled the trigger. Back to back, but his gun was on empty. "Fuck." He kicked the kid so hard she rolled under the bed. "Let's go, nigga. The safe back here." He rushed out of that room and into the room next to it. Pushed open the closet door and moved a bunch of stuff out of the way before he drug out a small safe that looked like a mini refrigerator.

I stood shaking like a leaf while he punched in a digital code, then pulled it open. He took a black garbage bag out of his drawers and flipped it out. Then, he started filling it with money, just as the doorbell started to ring.

I damn near fainted. My legs got so weak that I had to hold on to the wall. This was three murders already, and the baby that had at once been screaming was now silent. I worried that bruh had killed her as well. Now there was somebody ringing the doorbell. I was so paranoid that I was seeing stars.

Juelz continued to fill the bag with money until the safe was empty. Then he jumped up. "Let's go out the back, side door, bruh. Come on." He rushed out of the room and ran down the hallway at full speed.

When we got to the stairs both of us almost fell down them because we were in such a haste. But we kept our balance and made it out of there, and back to his truck with me feeling like I was sick.

Juelz jumped in and pulled away from the curb, laughing at the top of his lungs. "That's how you do that shit, nigga. You smoke somethin', get in, and get the fuck out. Fuck them Yankees. That's sixty gees on top of this fifty in this bag. What a night. And we still ain't finished. Let's get it." He pulled off of the block.

I sat back in my seat trying to gather myself. The murders kept on replaying in my head.

The female, then the two dudes. I worried if the baby had been killed along with them. I wondered how karma was going to get me back. Us back. I felt like the souls were already haunting me. "Bruh, you sure that hitting another lick is the right move tonight? I mean that bag will compensate for the two niggas we didn't hit up, right?"

He sucked his teeth. "Hell n'all. That ain't how the game go. I was sent on a mission. I gotta handle all five of these bodies. Once you're given a misson, you can't pick and choose how much of the mission you're going to carry out. That'll get me and my whole family killed. Besides, you gotta get some blood on your hands. This ain't sweet." He mugged me, then looked off.

I swallowed. I already figured that. There was no way I was going to be able to get through the night without bodying at least one person. Juelz gave me a look that said he was already disappointed, but I didn't give a fuck. All of this was new to me. I hadn't killed before, and I was sure I would have stanked the dude that I was supposed to, but he was holding a newborn baby. That was a clear path to hell.

"Look, bruh, it's two Puerto Rican bandits that we gotta lay down. They gon' be at this bar over on Ashland. We gon' keep this shit short and sweet. Gon' run in that bitch, and you gon' blast both of them. Noodle shots. Kill them, and we up out of that bitch. You can keep fifty thousand of this bag, and I'ma throw you another ten. That's sixty even. Cool?"

I nodded and exhaled loudly. "Cool."

* * *

I kept my back against the side of the building as I eyed the door to the tavern across the narrow street. Juelz had went inside of it only a minute earlier. I was waiting for him to come out of it and give me the signal so I could do my thing. I was saying a silent prayer in my head, asking for forgiveness. My mind was already made up. I was going to do what I had to. For one, I needed the money, and two, well I didn't really have a choice. I was in too deep. I stood there trying to shake the jitters out as a big raccoon crawled out of the alley and headed toward me with its eyes lit up the color of electricity. I stomped my foot at it and stopped. It stood up on and clasped its fingers within one another. That shit spooked me. I ain't like animals at all. Especially ones that had hands like people. That freaked me out.

Juelz stepped out of the door to the tavern and lit a cigarette. That was the signal. As soon as I saw that I braced myself and dashed across the street, heading for the front door.

"Both of them got green rags around their necks. Handle that and come on." He continued to puff on his cigarette. "They the only two sitting at the bar. Go."

I grabbed the handle to the door with my pistols already cocked. Threw it open, and rushed in. The bar was packed with at least twenty patrons. There was Mariachi music coming out of the speakers. It smelled like tobacco and musk. My eyes went to the bar where there were two Spanish dudes sitting with green rags around their necks. On each side of them was a female that looked as if they were involved in some stimulating conversations. The sight of the women nearly made me want to pull back from handling my business, but I was sure that if I had that me and Juelz would have fallen out. He'd made it perfectly clear what the stakes were. So instead of retreating, I upped my gun and rushed the foursome. One of the females jumped up with her eyes wide. I aimed at the man she'd been talking to and pulled the trigger three times, giving him facials. He flew off of the bench and landed on the floor leaking.

His girl screamed at the top of her lungs. His guy jumped up and pulled out a chrome .45. I sent two shots into his neck. His head jerked on his shoulders before he fell face-first, dropping his gun. I stood over him and let two more shots off into his body with my gun jumping in my hands before I ran out of the tavern, back across the street along the side of the building I'd been standing while I waited for Juelz previously. I saw that the raccoon looked as if it had been stomped to death. I ran past it into the alley, where Juelz was waiting in the truck for me.

"Let's go, nigga. That shit done."

He nodded. "That's what's up. Now it's time to get money."

Chapter 12

I was so fucked up from that night that I didn't wind up getting up with Punkin. I locked myself away in Miss Jackie's guest bedroom for two days. Then Sodi came over on her birthday and insisted that we spend some time together. At this time, I was still sick over the murders. I was having crazy nightmares, and seeing their souls chasing me every time I closed my eyes. Killing somebody had turned out to be way harder than I'd thought. Pulling the trigger had been easy, but the remorse afterward was the hardest thing ever. At least that's how I felt.

Miss Jackie knocked on the door two times, then opened it; stuck her head in the room. "Hey, baby, I know you said that you needed to be alone for a few days, but this lil' girl insisting that you see her. You want me to let her in?"

I sat up in bed and paused the movie I was watching. "Who is it?" I was hoping she was going to say my sister. Marie had hit my phone two days prior saying that she was okay, and that I shouldn't worry about her. Then she hung up the phone. That was the last time I'd heard from her.

"That Spanish girl with the butt. Uh, Saudi, or Sodi. Whatever." I didn't know if she'd messed up on her name on purpose, or if it was accidental. Either way, I needed to see her. I needed to take my mind off of the murders.

"Yeah, mama, let her come in. It's good." I got out of the bed and tossed a white beater on. By the time Sodi came into the room I was halfway decent.

"Damn, what's good with you?" she asked looking all made up. She looked like a finer version of Kim K before she had all of that plastic surgery shit. And her ass was just as fat.

I came around the bed and hugged her. "I been chilling. Why? What's the matter?" She sort of cringed in my arms, so I knew that something was wrong.

She stepped out of my embrace and mugged me. "I ain't seen you in two weeks. You ain't texted, nor called me. Ain't inboxed me. I'm pissed. You could have least sent me a happy birthday." She looked angrier than I have ever seen her.

I lowered my head and ran my hand over my waves. "Damn, I'm bugging. That's my bad. I been going through some thangs." I plopped on the bed and closed my eyes. More images of the murder scene played over in my mind. I hurried and opened my eyes.

"TJ, I don't want to make this about you. It's my day. I want today to be about me. So, it's four in the afternoon, and you're going to take me out on the town. I already got a limo that you're goin' to pay for. Then you're going to take me to a nice dinner, and then after that I'ma give you my virginity. I don't know why I am, but I am. Get ready. I'll be waiting outside." She opened the door to my bedroom and turned her back to me. I caught a glimpse of that big ass booty that was stuffed in a tight Gucci skirt dress and knew that I was going do everything that she told me to. I wanted to be the first nigga to slide into that body. I didn't really know if I believed that I would be her first, but I was definitely looking forward to finding out.

* * *

Sodi had rented a stretch Lincoln Town Car limo. It was all black with the white interior. They wanted three hundred for six hours and I was cool with that. It came equipped with a bottle of Moet that would cost me extra, but it was cool; it was her day. I slid into the backseat fitted in a black and red Gucci suit, with the matching Retro Jordan's. Had a diamond stud in each ear, and a nice gold Movado on my left wrist, with the Gucci shades. I was styling and feeling a bit better. Now I needed to get into my mode so I could get on her level emotionally.

She cuddled under my right arm and kissed my cheek. She smelled like a Puerto Rican blessing. I think I found her so fine because her skin was dark like a sista's, but she had those real Spanish features. It was crazy. "Damn, TJ, how long is it gon' take before you tell me how good I look?" She rubbed my arm and smiled.

"Yo, you look super bad tonight, baby, and you smell just as good. I'm sorry. I been slipping lately, especially on your day, but I'ma make it up to you. That's my word." I tilted her head up and kissed her soft lips. They felt like the petals of a rose. I had a thing for this woman. I couldn't lie.

She batted her eyelashes at me and exhaled, shaking her head. "TJ, do you care about me? Like, do you honestly have any feelings for me at all?"

I cleared my throat. That question had caught me off guard. "Why you ask me that, Sodi?" I was trying to buy time because I honestly didn't know how to answer that question. I mean I did care about her. But I didn't know if I was supposed to tell her that. I thought it would make me seem weak or soft. My father had never expressed his love and care to my mother, or any of us. So, I didn't know if I was supposed to let my feelings be heard, or verbally expressed. I was confused.

"I'm just asking because it doesn't seem like it. You're staying at a woman's house who you're clearly screwing. You and I haven't even been together in that way since you've been home. You never call, nor hit me up. You forget everything. And you never tell me that you care about me, so I just gotta know. Do you?"

I nodded. "Yeah. I care about you, and I got a lot of respect for you. I'm just trying to figure my life out right now. This whole thing with my sister and mother is killing me. My head is fucked up. I feel so alone. Straight up."

"You're only alone because it's how you choose to be. There is nothing that you can't come to me about. I been feeling you since forever. And it ain't take nothing for me to cross over to you. I been trying my best to hold you down ever since we became a part of one another. And you ain't never did nothing to show me that you even care about me. I'm still hooked on your selfish ass. I don't even understand it. I never will." She tried to break away from me as if she was mentally envisioning what she'd said out loud and it made her feel some type of way for the negative. I knew where she was coming from, and I disliked that I made her feel so less than. I could have been better in how I treated her. She had been the only female, besides Miss Jackie, that had stood by me while I was on lock. That meant the world to me.

I pulled her back into my arms snugger, resting my lips against the side of her forehead. "I'm sorry, Sodi, you're right. I got real bad trust issues. I been through a lot in my life. My family is crazy, so I was raised crazy, and to trust nothing or body. I couldn't show any emotion in our household without being pounced on, so I'm still not good at doing it right now." I paused and one of the more severe beatings that I had taken from my father came into my mind.

He'd caught me consoling my sister one day after she'd ran into the end table. I had to be about eight years old, and she was four. This was one of those times that I had never seen her cry so hard, or so loud. But I rushed to her to assess the damage that she'd done to her side. When I saw that the end table had poked through her skin, and that she was bleeding pretty bad, it made me cry because it was like I could feel her pain. Not only that but she was my baby sister. I never liked to hear her cry or see her in pain. I knew even back then that it was my job to protect her. When my father came out of the back room and saw me hugging her, with tears coming down my cheeks, he grabbed an extension cord and beat me for fifteen minutes straight, then put me on punishment for a month. He said that boys weren't supposed to cry. That emotions were for bitches.

Sodi shook me out my fog. "Baby. Baby. Where did you just go? Your eyes were bucked, and you seemed like you were in a zone."

I shook my head. "Anyway, I'm sorry, baby. I'ma get better at trying to open up more to you. But we also gotta get to know each other a little better. I mean, I know you through letters and phone calls, but I want to know the physical you." I saw that the Limo had entered downtown.

The big buildings were all around us lit up. It was a clear night. Even though I had the murders going through my head I felt like I was in a serene place with Sodi. It was all I wanted to think about. The weight of the world was getting me down, and I was trying my best to not succumb to the tornado of my reality. I didn't want to be swallowed up and spat out into a dark, sunken place.

We wound up at a nice Italian restaurant by the name of Demetri's. Four star. It was quiet. Dimly lit. We picked a table right by the big window so we could look out at the big lake outside of the restaurant. After ordering our food we gave our menus back to the Maître D, and Sodi reached across the table and took my hand into hers. "Baby, my life is just as crazy as yours. My father is absent. My mother works two fulltime jobs, and two part time ones. I have ten siblings, and all of them are younger than me, except for my older brother. He calls it for the Latin Kings over on Twenty-Sixth and California. Well, that whole hood, really." She blew air out of her jaws. "I want to go to college so I can become a veterinarian, but I don't want to leave my mother alone to care for my siblings. My father doesn't care about us at all. The last time I spent some time with him, he tried to force himself upon me, and made it seem as if I owed him some. He's a heavy drinker, and I don't know... I just like to make it seem as if he isn't even alive." She looked into her lap. "I sound pretty screwed up, huh?"

I slid around the booth and placed my arm around her shoulder. "N'all, Mami, you sound like you were raised in Chicago. Both of us got secrets and pains. The question I want to know is how can you be so young and you're trying to hold me down the way that you are? What is it about me? And what can I do to help you with your situation?"

She shrugged. "I just like you, TJ. I think you're really fine. I like the way you carry yourself, and I believe that you're different. I can't help but to think that you're selfless. I remember what you did for Punkin when Blue tried to rape her, and I heard through the grapevine why you got locked up. Wasn't it because your father had beaten your mother pretty severely?" She looked up at me with concerned eyes.

I nodded. "Yeah, I wish I would have killed him that night. That fool waited until I got arrested and then started to go in on my sister. Him and my brothers. I don't know why I just exposed that to you, but it's out there now."

The Maître D came and set our plates of Lasagna on the table, along with garlic bread, our drinks, then bowed and walked away.

Sodi rubbed the side of my face and peered into my eyes. "It's good, TJ. Maybe you know that you can trust me. I mean I just told you what happened with me and my father, but what I didn't tell you is that he actually did some things to me throughout my childhood that makes me sick to my stomach. I mean, I won't go into any details, but let's just say for a long time I hated myself." She shook her head and laid it on my shoulder. "I feel so alone though. It's like the older I become the smarter I am. Life is really fucked up. Like this world is so cold. So full of hate. It's no longer about Black, white, or Spanish, it's about Have and Have-nots, and when you're a Have-not like us, the world hates you. I'm so tired. No matter how much my mother works, we're still dirt poor. I mean, my brother does what he can, but my mother won't accept his drug money. She says that she'd rather starve."

"That's messed up. But I see it ain't stopping you from accepting his paper. Every time I see you, you're fitted in designer. I ain't mad at you either." I laughed and hugged her tighter to me.

"They're just clothes, TJ. I am more than fabric. I still ain't got no money in my purse. I don't know how I'm going to pay for college, so that I can get an education, get a good job and take some of the load off of my mother. Every day I feel like I'm going to die, and I might as well tell you everything. I'm addicted to these." She reached into her bag and flashed a small sandwich bag with about ten pills inside of it.

"What's that?" I snatched it out of her hand and looked them over closely. "These Oxys?" I mugged her.

She nodded. "Yeah. I got a thing for Perks too. Anytime I feel like life is becoming too much, I pop a few pills. They make me feel better. Give my stuff back." She held out her hand.

I slid them across the table and shrugged. "Shit, we all got our vices. I ain't gon' judge you about yours."

She smiled and replaced them. "Thank you. I would appreciate if you didn't. Gon' round to your side of the table now before this stuff gets cold."

I did just that, and for the next ten minutes we sat there maxing our food. I kept looking across the table at her and liking the sights of her. Sodi was bad as hell. I had to find a way to lay her down. I knew she had to have a shot on her.

"TJ, am I your girl, or are we just really good friends? Be honest." She picked up her glass of pop, sipping from it.

I finished chewing the mouthful of food that I had and picked up my pop. My hands were greasy from the garlic bread, so I almost dropped it, but I gathered myself quick, and got me a few swallows while I tried to peep the game she was slinging at me. I set the glass back down. "I think we still need to get to know each other a little better before we make anything official. I know that I care about you though, and I want to find a way that I can help you in this life, period. I mean I ain't got everything for myself figured out yet, but I feel like I will soon. But you are my girl. I just don't know to what extent."

"Is it to the extent that I'ma lay down and give you some birthday sex?" She asked dropping her fork, mugging me with anger.

"Not if you ain't comfortable with that. I ain't trying to pressure you into doing anything. I'd be perfectly fine with just holding you tonight. I gotta be with you. You are important to me." I felt like I was losing my window to get some of that pussy, and I wasn't trying to do that. I'd known her for a long time, and I'd never gotten the chance to get between them legs.

"You know what, TJ? You're full of shit. Nigga, I know ya' ass don't care about me. No nigga does. All of you men are the same. Y'all only care about who you're fucking in the moment. I will bet you any money that had we have fucked by now that you would have never been able to go weeks at a time without responding to my messages or getting up with me. That's why you're over there with that old chick. It's because she's breaking you off what I haven't been. But if that's what it's going to take for you to mess with me on that level, then let's go. Let's just get this shit over with." She scooted away from the table and threw the napkin that had been in her lap on top of her lasagna.

I sat there for a second, then pulled out a knot of cash. Paid the bill and left a ten percent tip.

Chapter 13

I sat on the edge of the hotel bed, and turned up the bottle of Ace of Spades, then set it on the night table beside the bed.

Sodi came out of the bathroom with her tight skirt still clung to her body, but her long, silky hair fell all over her chest and arms. She walked over until she was standing in front of me, right between my legs. "Do you really want me, TJ? Huh?" Her eyes looked into mine, almost challenging.

I nodded, and looked down to her pretty toes, all the way back to her dime face. "Hell yeah, I do. I been wanting you since day one." I reached out for her.

She moved my hands out of the way and took a step back. "TJ, I'm not like those other females. If I give myself to you, I am going to be a problem. I love so hard. Do you understand that?" Her eyes got watery. She wiped a lone tear away.

Now I was starting to feel kind of bad. "Look, Ma, we ain't gotta do this if you don't want to. I mean, I'd be perfectly fine with just holding you like I said before. I mean, it is your day today, and it ain't just about the pussy for me. I genuinely care about you." Now I was serious. As I looked her over, I saw so much pain in her eyes. She was shaking just a bit, as if she was cold, or on the verge of breaking down. I got up from the bed and came toward her.

She took another step back. "Ain't no nigga trying to mess with a female if she ain't fucking. I know how it is in Chicago. That's why it was so easy for me to wait on you, even though I ain't really know you that good. It's because I saw what you did for Punkin, then to your father because of what he'd done to your mother, and I just felt you were different. Then once you started to write me and say the things that you did, well, you just made me feel so special. So, I really need to know that if I give myself to you, that you're going to be with me. I am not strong enough to be hurt. My life is already in shambles, so please be honest."

I stepped toward her. This time she didn't move backward. Allowed for me to grab her shoulders. "Baby, I'ma be with you right now. We ain't gotta do this tonight. Just let me hold you. Let me heal you in any way that I can. I can tell that somethin' ain't right with you right now." I leaned my head and kissed her forehead, then hugged her close to me. The feel of her soft, warm body in my embrace made me feel strong and weak at the same time. The scent of her perfume drifted up my nose.

She allowed for me to hold her for a minute, then shook her head and wiggled out of my embrace. "N'all, Papi, I wanna do this. I just want to get this over with so we can move forward. The only thing I'm saying is that I want you to really see me after we're done doing this. Don't look at me as if I'm just one of these average bitches. I want you to see me as a queen. Do you think you'll be able to see me in that light?" She sucked on her bottom lip, then released it. It was nice and shiny.

I nodded. "Yeah, baby. I can. I already do. Come here." I walked up to her, and she pushed me back on the bed. "What's good?"

"Nothin', I just want you to take me in, that's all." She rolled her eyes, then reached down to the hem of her skirt, pulling it up her thighs. A pair if red lace panties came into view. They were all up in her crease. The skirt sailed past her stomach, then over her head. She dropped it on the floor and kicked it to the side. Stood before me in just her bra and panties. Her long hair cascading down her back.

"Well?" I reached out for her. "Come here. Let me take you in."

She stepped up to me and turned around. The panties were all up in her ass cheeks. Both golden globes were exposed. "I just want you to love me, TJ. Somebody has to love me. I feel so lost right now." She turned back and face me. Held the right side of my face in her right hand.

"Baby, what are you looking for? What do you want from me? I need to know this." I wanted her body, but I needed to know what it was going to cost me. She seemed to be so broken. I wanted to be there for her in any way that I could, beyond the physical aspect of my need for her.

"I don't know, TJ. I swear to God, I don't know. I think I just want you to love me, so I won't be so alone. I just wanna know that after we lay down that you won't emerge and leave me behind. I want to be a part of you from this night on out. Is that too much to ask?"

I shook my head. "N'all, baby, it ain't." I guess I understood her for the most part. The world really did suck when you had to fight in it alone. Being that she felt she had her little siblings, and her mother on her shoulder, I suppose it was weighing her down and this was her way of asking for help. I got that, and I was willing to step up to the plate.

"Well, take me then. I'm yours. Just remember you're taking all of me?" She kissed my lips real soft. Moved her head back to look into my eyes, staring at me. "You okay ,baby?"

I nodded and slid my hand around her small waist. Cuffed that big booty and squeezed it. Stood up and guided her to the bed. Once there, I bent between her thighs, and opened them wide. Sniffing the crotch band of her panties.

There was a hint of her kitty, and it was enough to make me lick up and down the material, until she was moaning, and opening her legs wider. "TJ, I love you. I hope you know that. Please know that."

I moved the band to the side, exposing her bald lips. I licked the right one and sucked it into my mouth. Moved the material all the way out of my way, so I could see her full mound. It was golden colored; the lips darker than the rest of her skin. They were engorged, and there was dew all of over them. The sight turned me on so much, that I opened them with my thumbs, and licked up and down her slit. Slurping her juices and manipulating her clit. This drove her crazy.

She bucked from the bed and threw her head back. Slid her right hand into her lap, trying to get at her box. "TJ, I'm so horny. Please take me, baby. Please. I'm aching." She attempted to touch her clit, but I moved her hand away. She groaned in frustration.

"I got this, Mami. Let me handle my business." I wrapped both of my lips around her clit and sucked hard. Slid a finger into her tight little hole, working it in and out. She was already so wet that there was a puddle under her golden ass cheeks.

"Un! TJ. Please. Fuck, Papi. That feel so. Uh!" She moaned, humping my face, after laying on her back.

I started making all kinds of loud nasty noise. Slurping her juices, and nipping her clit with my teeth, then sucking them lips into my mouth. Her juices ran all down my neck, and only encouraged me to go harder. I sucked two fingers into my mouth, slid them into her tight box, working them vigorously while I sucked her pearl tongue as if it were a nipple, and the gateway to her milk. My tongue ran circles around it.

She sat all the way up and screamed. Bucked into my face, and came hard, messing up my waves. "Papi. Papi. Oh, it feel so good. Get up here. I need you." She reached for me, shaking as if she was freezing.

I licked and sucked all over her exposed thigh. Pulled her panties down her thighs and off of her ankles. Then I kissed her pretty toes. One at a time. They were small and painted to match the Gucci fit she'd worn. I took my time and kissed, then sucked each individual toe into my mouth, before switching to the next foot. For me there was nothing like a female with some small feet and pretty toes, and hers were just that. Size sevens, and freshly pedicured. While I sucked her toes, she played with her kitty. Rubbing a lone finger up and down in between her lips. Moaning loudly. I sucked up her ankle, and along her inner thigh. Moved her finger out of the way and kissed all over her pretty pussy. The lips were wet and swollen.

"Papi, get yo' ass up here and give me some. Please, while I'm not scared to do it." She rubbed all over my head and the back of my neck, opening her thick thighs wider.

"Let me see it again." I swallowed the juices that were in my mouth, and took a step back, smacking my lips together. Slid my shirt over my head, along with the beater, and dropped it to the floor. Then undid my belt and pants. Allowed them to slide to my feet as well. My dick was sticking up like a baseball, pitching a tent in my boxers. I hooked my fingers inside of them and slid them to the floor. Wrapped my right fist around my pipe, and stroked it a few times, then took it away. Leaving it jumping up and down. Fully engorged, and dark brown. "You ready for me, Mami? Huh?" I stepped toward her.

Her eyes were bugged out of her head. When I got close enough, she reached out and grabbed it. Pulled me to her, then started to stroke it up and down. Running her tongue over her lips. "I wanna taste you, Papi. I forgot how you taste." She licked my head, then sucked me into her mouth, taking me inch by inch until her nose was pressed against my lower abs. It felt hot and wet. Her little fist struggled to close around my girth.

"Do it, Mami. Make Papi feel good. Fuck." I guided her head up and down faster and faster. My eyes were wide open. I didn't wanna miss a beat of this bad female doing her thing to me.

Very little things were hotter than a dime sucking your dick. That's how I felt. Sodi was super fine, and she was deep throating me like a porn star. I felt like I'd hit the jackpot. I humped into her mouth, feeling like I was on the verge of cumming. Reached over her back and gripped her ass. Played in between the crack, all the way down to her pussy, and opened the lips. At the feel of them, I came in her mouth. Jerking. She kept right on sucking me faster and faster, moaning all around the head, sucking it like a lemon. Making me moan like a broad. Once she saw that I was done cumming, she started stroking me with her mouth still over the head. This allowed for me to get harder than I was before.

She popped her mouth off of it. "Okay, come on now, Papi. I want you to be the first man besides my dad to ever get into me. Please. I need you to heal me and erase him." She scooted back on the bed. I couldn't take my eyes from in between her legs. Her pussy was so fat.

The comment she'd made about her father stung me a little bit, but it really didn't get to me like that. Chicago was so crazy that I didn't put anything past anybody. Life was life, and it was what it was. I wanted some of that pussy, and I was going for it.

I jumped on the bed and crawled between her legs. Opened them wide and lined myself up. The big head right on her dripping hole. Her cream overflowed out of her hole as if it were lava. The juices ran into her ass crack. Everything down there was glowing. I pulled my dick back and licked all over her lowers. Sucked the lips again, then repositioned myself. "Here we go, baby. You ready?" I slowly started to enter her.

"Wait, TJ. Tell me you love me, please. I just want to hear it one time. Please. I've never done this and had that said to me. So, please, baby." I had about two inches inside of her and her pussy was sucking at me. It was so hot, and tight. Like she had an oven down there.

To be able to slide all the way inside of her, I probably would have said anything. I didn't know if I really loved her or not, but I knew what was needed to be heard in order for our coupling to progress. I wanted Sodi way too bad to worry about the logistics of things. "I love you, Mami. I love you, and I'ma hold you down. I promise."

Her eyes teared up quick and spilled over. She pulled me on top of her and dug her nails into my back. "Do it, Papi. Do it good. I'm yours."

I cocked back and slid all the way forward, slamming my piece as deep into her as I could go. My face rested in the crux of her neck. "Damn, Sodi, this pussy fye." I cocked back and slammed home again, then I was stroking it like a pro with her juices pooling out of her. A constant smacking sound occurred from between our legs.

Her nails dug into my back and tore the skin there, but I didn't care. Her cat had me thirsty for more of it. "Uh, Papi. Shit, Papi. You're my daddy now. You're my daddy now. Say it, Papi. Uh! Fuck, say it." She pulled her bra over her breasts, exposing her hard nipples that stood out an inch a piece. The areolas looked like pacifiers.

I pushed them together and sucked back and forth from one nipple to the other. "I'm Daddy. I'm Daddy. You my baby. This pussy belong to me now." I fucked her harder and harder, long-stroking that box.

She got wetter and wetter. "Uh, Daddy. Don't say that. Fuck. Don't talk to me like that." Her nails dug into my back, then she was rubbing up and down it. Moaning loud. Sucking on my neck. "Tell me you love me, Daddy. Tell me you love me and only me."

I sped up the pace. The bed rocked back and forth, beating on the wall. A pillow fell off of the bed as I grabbed her hips and pulled her closer to me, so I could really dig into her middle. "Daddy love you. Daddy love baby. Fuck, I love you."

She arched her back and screamed before cumming all over my pole, shaking like crazy. "Daddy. You're my daddy. Fuck." She scooted back and got on all fours with that round ass in the air. Her pussy's lips were slightly opened. I could see the pink of her insides. Her cream ran down to her thighs. "You gotta fuck me like this. He used to always wanna do me from behind. I need you to erase that, Papi. Hurry up." She spread her knees apart.

I kissed her right on her asshole and licked around it, then slid into her from the back. Gripped the skin of her hips and started to fuck her so hard that I was hurting myself, but it felt so good. From the back I was able to get all up in her tunnel. Her big booty crashed into my stomach and jiggled. Her long hair was all over her face. She came after the twentieth stroke and fell forward with me still working that ass.

"You're my daddy. You're my daddy. You're my daddy. Uh. You're my daddy now. I love you. I love you so much." She came again and was shaking so bad that it worried me. It ain't stop me from piping her or nothing, but I was worried. I came when she looked back at me with her curly hair all over her face.

That was one of the sexiest sights I had ever seen, and it was too much for me to handle. I collapsed against her ass and started to lick all over her neck, breathing hard. Fifteen minutes later, we'd showered, used the bathroom, and laid cuddled up together with me spooning her naked, and rubbing all over her right thigh and booty cheek.

She had a smile on her face with her eyes closed. "TJ, that was amazing. I feel so much better. How about you, Papi?"

I felt like a businessman that had just moved up in the company. "I feel good too, boo. You got that good-good between these thighs. I wasn't expecting all of that." I slid my hand between her closed thighs and rested it on her pussy. Playing with the lips.

She moaned. "Well, I guess I'll take that as a compliment. But I hope you know that I am more than sex. I want to be your Queen. I love you for real. I don't care how early it is to be saying that. I need you."

I kissed the back of her neck. "Baby, when you don't have nothing, you're forced to hold on tight to whatever you do have. We need each other. I love you, too. I mean I may not be where you are as deep yet, but I will be. I just got so much going on. I need to find my sister." Now that I'd cum, and that part of my anatomy was taken care of, I was starting to remember my reality.

Sodi turned all the way around until she was facing me. "What are you going to do when you find her?"

I shrugged. "I don't know yet. I think I'ma get her up out of Chicago because this city is killing her. But before I do that, whatever nigga that got her, I'ma make his ass pay tenfold. I'm very serious. She's only fourteen. Got grown niggas passing her around as if she's a toy or something. That shit make me sick to my stomach."

Sodi took a deep breath and slid out of the bed. Stood before me in all of her sexy, naked glory. Her titties looked perfect in the light. The brown nipples covered a nice portion of her mounds. "Baby, remember that I told you that my brother call shots for the Kings on the westside?" She flipped a tuft of hair over her shoulders.

I sat up. My piece slapping into my thigh. "Yeah, what about it?" I looked her over closely.

She looked nervous, biting on her index fingernail. "Well, my brother Jorge does business with your brother Deion on the cocaine side, and he told me that when he was over there yesterday, that he saw your sister sitting on the couch next to Deion, getting high. Baby, I think your sister is at your brother's trap. I think that's where she stays."

I slid out of the bed and stood up, rushed around the bed and grabbed a handful of her hair. "Ma, why you ain't tell me that shit? Huh? Why the fuck you wait this long to tell me!"

Instead of screaming or trying to fight against me, she remained calm. "Daddy, I was wrong. You're right. I'm sorry, but I'm tellin' you now. That's where she is. I guess I wanted to spend some time with you before you went off on some rampage. Now please unhand me." She remained hunched over, calm. Her long hair touching the floor. Tickling my toes.

I released her and exhaled loudly. "Damn, Sodi. If me and you about to be one hunnit with each other, you gotta keep shit real with me at all times. Don't be keeping stuff from me, especially when it involves my people."

"I'm sorry, Papi. I was just on some selfish, attention-needing shit. It's been hard for me too. Please don't be mad. I beg of you." She blinked and tears ran down her cheeks.

I pulled her to me and wrapped her in my arms. "It's good, Boo, come here." I held her, feeling my piece mold to her hot skin. "You know which trap your brother was talking about?"

She shook her head. "N'all, and my brother won't tell me, but I do know where his baby mother stay. He's been real bogus toward her. She been all on Facebook with their drama. Supposedly he screwed her cousin and got her best friend pregnant at the same time that she is. It's nuts. She used to go to our school, but I think she was a few grades under me. Her name is Jelissa."

Chapter 14

"If I was you, I'd just go in there busting, god. Word up. Your brother one of them arrogant, evil niggas. He don't respond to nothing but violence. Nine times out of ten, his bitch gon' be the same way. I think Shorty from the east coast too, and them hoes back there ain't nothin' nice. Word up." Juelz said, as he bended the corner to Deion's baby mother's crib. The block was already packed with people. Before he could turn all the way on to it, we were stopped by a bunch of females. They waved us away and started to put up barricades.

I rolled down the window. "Fuck y'all out here doing, Shorty?"

A dark skinned sista with some thick thighs walked up to Juelz's truck. "We about to have a block party. Ain't no cars can be parked on the block from now until ten o'clock tonight. Sorry, y'all gotta keep it moving." Then she walked off with her shorts all up in her ass.

Juelz slammed his fists on the steering wheel. "Fuck." He looked around and saw more and more people setting up for the party. "It's good though, I'm just gon' pull around through the alley. We'll go from there. It's more than one way to skin a cat."

So that's what we did. He parked directly behind her crib, and we walked alongside of her gangway until we got to her porch. Once there, I rang the doorbell three times and waited. It appeared that all of the other people on the block were coming out of their homes to help set up. They were carrying tables, speakers, sound systems, and food. It had to be about eighty degrees out, sunny, with a slight breeze. I saw a lot of kids filling up their water guns, preparing for a water war.

Jelissa came to the door, two minutes after we'd rang the bell. I could see her through the screen door. She looked to be about 5'4", slim, with a real pretty face, and these juicy lips that were shined with lip gloss. She didn't look a day over fifteen, and what really threw me off was when she opened her mouth and began talking all proper. "Excuse me. May I help you two?" She asked, opening the screen door. She had a nice perfume on.

I nodded my approval at that. The smell of a woman was important no matter who they were. "Yeah, Shorty, I'm looking—"

She cut me off. "My name is not Shorty, it's Jelissa. And before anything else, who are you, and who are you looking for?"

Juelz started to bump me out of the way. "Bitch, where the fuck yo' baby daddy punk ass at? Word up. We ain't got no time for this back and forth."

I bumped him. "Chill, nigga, it's good. I got this." She looked offended. "Sorry about all that, but I'm looking for my brother Deion. I gotta holler at him about my little sister. Do you know where I can find him?"

She placed her hand on her little hip and shook her head. "No, I do not, and if I did, just by the way your mans came at me I wouldn't tell you anything anyway. Y'all need to leave my porch." She started to close the door.

I grabbed it and stopped her. "Look, Marie my sister. She doing them drugs real tough and bruh ain't trying to help her get off of them. All I want is my little sister. That's all. I'm worried about her." I was trying my best to be humble. I was seconds away from snatching her lil' ass up. The only thing that was preventing me from doing that was because I could see the little pooch in her middle. That confirmed to me that she was pregnant. So, on that strength alone I was giving her a polite pass.

"Look, that's screwed up, but it's not my business. I ain't got nothing to do with that. Y'all gon' have to find him on your own. That's just that. Now, I'ma ask y'all one more time to leave my porch. If you don't, I'ma—"

Juelz snatched her by the throat and led her back into the house. He picked her up off of her feet and walked with her. I stepped into the house behind him and closed the door. Watched him throw her to the couch and pull out his pistol. He cocked it back and placed it against her cheek. "Bitch, where the fuck that nigga at? This yo' last warning before I put two in ya' melon."

She looked up at him and frowned. "Like I said, that ain't my business to tell, so you gon' have to do what you have to. I just hope he know, over there, that I'm pregnant with his brother's baby." She eyed me and ignored Juelz.

Juelz grabbed a pillow from the couch and placed it over her face. "Man, fuck this bitch, B. She think shit sweet. I'm finna bam her ass." He cocked the hammer.

My conscious got the better of me. I couldn't let him kill an innocent, pregnant female. I placed my hand on top of his gun. "N'all, bruh, give her a pass. She ain't who we looking for." I pulled the pillow off of her face. "Shorty, that nigga gon' get you killed. You sitting there keeping your mouth closed, with one toe in the grave. What about your baby?" I was trying to talk some sense into her. She seemed real hard-headed.

She shrugged. "If it's meant to be, it will be. If not, then it is what it is."

There was the sound of heavy footsteps coming up the stairs outside. They stopped at the door, and then began picking with the lock. I pulled my pistol out now, and walked closer to the front door, trying to see who it was.

"You been looking for him, there he go. I wanna see y'all try all that tough shit with him."

The door swung inward and Deion stepped into the hallway with his arm around a female that looked like she was about seventeen. He walked all the way inside of the house with his face buried in her neck, didn't even notice that me and Juelz was in the house strapped and ready to dead his ass.

It took for JD, who was a few feet behind him to see us, and make him aware. "Yo, People! It's a hit!" He hollered and pulled his Glock from his waistband.

Deion's eyes got big. He threw the female at Juelz, upped two pistols, and aimed them both at Juelz. "What the fucks good, Juelz? What you doing here?"

Juelz tapped his trigger and enacted the red beam on top of his gun. Placed the beam on Deion's forehead, and frowned. "Bitch ass nigga, lower that gun, or get yo' shit pushed back."

I came closer to him with my gun aimed at JD. "Nigga, you know yo' soft ass ain't gon' bust shit. Put that gun down. I'd love to splash yo' sick ass." I walked all the way up on him and placed my barrel in his face. Itching to dump him.

He looked to Deion for what to do. "Man, ain't nobody even fuckin with you, TJ. Damn, stay in yo' lane."

"Nigga, on my mother, if you don't put that gun down, I'ma smoke you like a Newport." I cocked my hammer.

Deion shook his head. "Aiight, man. This shit ain't gotta go down like this. JD, lower your gun, and I'ma lower mine. They got the ups on us. It's all good." He put his guns back on his waistband. "Jelissa, bitch, I know you set me up. When these niggas leave, I'ma kick that baby out of yo' ass. On my Daddy life I am." He curled his upper lip.

"Deion, I swear to God I ain't have nothin' to do with this. They blindsided me too. They just got here a little before you did."

"Bitch, shut up. I said my peace," he growled. "Fuck y'all want with me?" He looked from me to Juelz.

 muffed JD with all of my might and knocked his bitch ass over. I always hated that. Reached down and took his pistol from him. That chump wasn't no killer. "Pussy ass nigga." Then stood up and placed my nose against Deion's. "Where the fuck my lil' sister at, you rapist ass nigga?"

He clenched his teeth. "She put up. That shit ain't got nothing to do with you. Stay in yo' lane. I run this shit."

My heart started to pound in my chest right away. "Bruh, on everything, don't play with me. Where the fuck is my baby sister?"

"Nigga, like I said, stay in yo' lane. I run this shit now, and that's what it is. She put up. You gon' do somethin', do it."

My temper got the best of me. I smacked him as hard as I could in the mouth with my pistol, knocking his two front teeth right out. He reached for his pistol, and I stole off on him with my left hand, in right in the eye. I mean I punched him hard, too. He flew backward and sat on his baby mother. Hopped up and rushed me with blood spewing from his mouth. Tackled me into the wall.

As soon as my back hit it, I brought my elbow down into the back of his head and flipped him off of me. He wound up on his back, groaning in pain. I kicked him as hard as I could in his ribs. "Where the fuck my sister at?" *Bam!* Kicked him again. He flipped over to his ribs.

JD looked as if he was about to rush me when Juelz jumped in front of him and smacked him with his right hand. "Fuck you think you finna do, nigga?"

JD fell to one knee and looked up at him with angry eyes. "You niggas gon' pay for this. I swear to God y'all is."

I grabbed Deion by the new growth of his dreads and pressed my gun to his cheek. "Where the fuck my sister at ,nigga? Huh?"

He lips were swollen. Split. Blood ran out of them. "You heard what I said before, nigga. You better pull that trigger if you know what's good for you." He coughed up a bloody loogey and spat it on the carpet beside him. I imagined me blowing his brains all over the carpet. Just ending his life and getting it over with.

The only thing that was stopping me from pulling the trigger is the fact that he was my brother, and I didn't know if I was mentally ready to have his murder on my conscious. The other niggas that me and Juelz had already killed were nightly torturing me. I was barely hanging on. If I'da added Deion's murder along with theirs, I was sure that I would not be able to keep my sanity.

"Fuck is you waiting on, nigga? Kill me! Kill me, because if I get up off of this floor, I'm damn sure gon' come back and kill both of you niggas. Watch." His teeth were bloodied red.

"Yo, kill that fuck boy, kid. Murk his punk ass. If you won't then I will!"

Jelissa screamed at the top of her lungs and rushed over, pushing me off of Deion. Then she laid out flat on top of him. "Please don't kill my baby daddy. Please. Just get out of my house!"

The other female that Deion had come in with, jumped up and ran to the back of the house. "Help! Help! They got guns in here!" She hollered.

Juelz took off behind her. JD kicked me as hard as he could in the side of my face and dazed me. I fell to my side. Deion got up and kicked me in the face, knocking me out cold. I didn't wake up until five minutes later. Juelz threw a glass of ice-cold water in my face and I jumped up in shock. I felt like I couldn't breathe. My jaw hurt.

"Yo, Kid, we gotta get the fuck out of here. That lil' bitch ran out the back door and I just know she gon' call the cops. Get yo' ass up. Let's bounce."

I slowly made my way to my feet. Staggered, and ran behind him. We hit it out the back door, and went back the way we'd once come. When we got back to Juelz's truck we found it stripped down and sitting on a bunch of bricks. The wheels were gone, and so were the doors, the system, the speakers, the engine, and the transmission. It was crazy. I couldn't believe my eyes. We had only been in there for about twenty minutes.

Juelz swung at the air. "Ain't this about a bitch! Who in the fuck?" He stopped and looked in both directions, pissed.

I was still trying to get my footing. My jaw felt like it was at the very least cracked. It hurt every time I tried to open my mouth in the slightest. I heard sirens and knew that we needed to get a move on. "Man, Blood, we gotta go. Twelve coming. I hear them sirens." I held my jaw as soon as I got done talking. It felt like I was being hit in the mouth with a sledgehammer.

Juelz looked at his truck again and seemed like he wanted to cry. "Yo, that's a Benz truck, my nigga. I ain't even get a chance to slap no insurance on that shit. Fuck, I hate Chicago! Let's go." He took off running just as a police car turned into the alley with its lights on

"Fuck." I broke right behind him, then branched off and hit a gangway. I already knew that if we got caught, the police wasn't gon' play no games with us.

This was Chicago. At the very least, whether you were innocent or not, they was whooping your ass and putting you in the hospital. So even though my jaw felt like it was about to come off, I was running as fast as I could through the back of somebody's yard. Once there I ran along the side of their house, and on to the next block. Ran across that street and was running through another gangway. I took my pistol and threw it on top of a balcony and kept running. Heard a cruiser slam on its brakes. Looked back and saw two police jump out of the car, running behind me at full speed.

"Freeze! Chicago P.D. Freeze, or we'll shoot!"

That lil' saying fucked me up in the head. Why the fuck would they threaten to shoot me for running? I wasn't posing any threat to them whatsoever. Chicago was a city of demons. It felt like ice was in my lungs. My stomach was cramping, and my jaw hurt. I looked over my shoulder and saw the police getting closer and closer to me. I was running out of somebody's back yard when two more police appeared, coming from the direction in which I was running. I stopped, ran left and tried to hop a fence but I was way too tired. I got to the top, and two of them grabbed me. Slammed me to the ground and started to whoop my ass.

* * *

They brought me back to Jelissa's crib, and held me against the gate so she could make a positive I.D. She came out of the house with one of the officer's arms around her neck. "Okay, ma'am, we know that this is one of them. All we need is for you to identify him and we'll take him to the station and book him on home invasion charges. Is that him?"

Jelissa shrugged his arm off of her. She looked at me for a long time. "N'all, that ain't one of them. They were both high yellow, and he's brown skinned. I'll never forget their faces."

A white female police officer walked up and squeezed my mouth. "Look at him. It has to be one of them. We found this son of a bitch fleeing from the scene." She mugged me and looked back to Jelissa. "He's already in our system."

The officer that at first had his arm around her neck stepped beside her, and in a soothing voice, tried to coax her into giving me up. "Come on, baby girl. It's him. You're just scared, and that's okay. But if you identify him, you'll never have to worry about his bum ass again. We'll deal with him."

Jelissa pulled skin from her juicy bottom lip with her teeth. "Look, man, it's not one of them. Let him go. I know who they are when I see them, and he ain't it." She looked into my eyes before turning her back and walking back into the house.

As soon as she did, the white female cop kneed me in the stomach and backhanded me. I fell to my knees, out of breath. She spat in my face. "Take his ass in anyway."

Chapter 15

They kept me locked up for three days, and then let me go. When I stepped out of the county jail, Sodi was waiting at the curb in Miss Jackie's Lexus truck. She ran to me at full speed and jumped into my arms. "Papi, I missed you so much. Oh, I hate them fucking cops. I just hate 'em." Her long hair was pulled back into a ponytail. She smelled like White Diamonds.

"I know, baby, but I'm good. Let's get up out of here." Man, the police had spent three days whooping my ass with an old ass phone book. Everything on me hurt. I felt like I needed a hug, but I wasn't about to tell her that. I had to act like it wasn't no big thang when in actuality I felt like a victim to the third degree. They'd whooped my ass for me being innocent so I could only imagine what they would have done had she told them that I had really been one of the culprits. I was so mad that I had visions of smoking a few Pigs and covering them with a dirty ass blanket. Pun intended.

Sodi jumped down. "Wait a minute, baby, because I gotta tell you something before you freak out." She looked over her shoulder toward the truck.

I tried to see what she was seeing. It was eleven o'clock at night, and we were on 26th and California— land of the deadly Latinos. They literally posted up and waited for oppositions to their gang to be released from Cook County Jail so they could murder them. I didn't want us to be taken for one of their enemies. I didn't have a pistol, and I was already fucked up from the Pigs whooping my ass. I wanted to get out of there. "Alright, baby, you can tell me in the truck. Why Miss Jackie let you roll her whip anyway? Y'all cool like that now?"

She reached and held my face. "Baby, Jelissa is in the car, and she is fucked up. Your brother tried to kill her. Seriously. She's lucky that she didn't lose her baby. Her other son is in there too."

I frowned. "Her other son? She got another kid already? She don't look that old." I rubber-necked to see what I could see. "Why she rolling with you?"

Sodi rubbed my face. "Baby, your father snapped out and beat your mother nearly to death. He left her in the hospital hanging on to an inch of her life."

"What? My mama! Man, fuck this! I'm tired of playin' games with these niggas. I'm tired of them putting their hands on my mother. Where is she now?" My eyes watered. I imagined my father beating my already sick mother and I nearly lost it. My knees felt weak.

"She's at the hospital, baby, and she's all screwed up." Sodi started to shed tears. "The doctors are giving her a week to live. I'm sorry, Papi. I'm here for you." She hugged me tight.

My head was spinning so fast that I nearly lost my footing and all of my body weight fell against her. But she held me up like a champion, and this wouldn't be the first, nor last time. "Get me to the hospital, Sodi. I gotta see my mother. I gotta see my mother right now." I nudged her away from me and rushed to the truck. When I got there, Jelissa straightened up. I jumped in and pulled my seatbelt around me, on autopilot.

Jelissa's head was as big as a pumpkin, and her face was swelled up as bad as my mother's used to be. She looked real bad. Her right eye was stuck shut. She held on to a little boy about the age of two. His brown eyes were wide open and staring. "I ain't no snitch, TJ. I would have never told them police on you or Juelz. Please don't think that I did."

"I know you didn't, Ma. It's good. I appreciate you for holding your tongue. Let me know if there is anything that I can do for you and I won't hesitate. That's my word." I said all of this without looking back at her. The sight of her was making me feel some type of way. I'd seen my mother reflect her face so many times. I was tired of those sights.

"Your brother did this to me. He beat me into the ground like this. Said I disgust him. That I tried to set him up for you to kill him. This ain't his first time doing this to me either. I need to get away. I'm so afraid." She started to bawl, and because she did, her son did as well.

I turned around to console the both of them. "Y'all, chill with all this crying. I ain't gon' let him hurt you no more, Jelissa. You got my word on that. Just please stop crying." She was reminding me of my mother. That was breaking my heart. Then when I actually thought about my mother I felt like breaking down again. I needed to see her. Needed to get rid of my brothers and my punk ass father. I hated them.

Sodi got into the truck and started it right away, pulling away from the curb. "TJ, visiting hours with your mother isn't until five in the morning. Do you want to go back to Miss Jackie's house so you can get changed; maybe take a shower or something?"

I nodded. "Yeah, that sound cool. I need to get this jail stink up off of me. What about Marie? Has anybody heard from her lately?" I looked over to Sodi with optimism.

She shook her head. "Not that I know of. She hasn't been on Facebook or Instagram lately. The last time she posted anything was two days ago. I'm sorry, Papi."

I hung my head. "Man, I wish I knew where that nigga kept my sister at. This shit fucking up my head." I rubbed my temple. Remembered there was a child in the car and re-minded myself that I needed to watch my mouth. That wasn't cool.

Jelissa said, "Four sixty-three, West One Hundred and Forty-fourth Street. Riverdale. Your sister is on a Hundred and Forty-fourth and Normal right now. I know that for a fact. Deion's sick ass has been screwing her like crazy. He beat the crap out of JD the other night because he tried too, then he went and did it. My mind was so blown that I said something about it. He snapped and beat me for saying somethin' about that, and for what had taken place with you and Juelz. But that's where she is."

"Baby, you want to go there now, or do you want to go home first?" Sodi asked, touching my arm with her little hand.

I sat there lost in thought, weighing my options. I didn't have a pistol on me, or a game plan. Just two women and a child. I wanted to see my mother so bad, and I felt weak. Now wouldn't have been the right time to confront him because I was sure that I was going to kill him and JD. "Jelissa, you sure she gone be there tomorrow, too?"

"Your father live right next door to that trap, so if she's not there, she'll be next door with him shooting up. That's a guarantee. I've been over there enough to know how they get down, and it's exactly how they do. I wish I had known you better when you came to my house the first time. I would have told you where your sister was, and what was going on. I honestly didn't know that Deion was screwing her. Had I known, I would never be pregnant with his kid right now." She lowered her head and shook it from left to right.

Sodi looked in the rear-view mirror. "Girl, you straight. Knowing is half the battle. If you knew better, you'd do better. Now that you know what's good, you just have to make better choices. But we're here for you. We got your back, you best believe that."

I nodded. "Yeah, lil' sis. It's all good. Me and my baby gon' hold you and your son down. What's his name, by the way?" I asked, looking down at the little boy that was snuggled into her.

She lowered her head to him. "His name if Rae'Jon. He's two years old, and he's all I have, besides my sister. Say hi, baby."

Rae'Jon looked up at me, then buried his head back into his mother's arm pit. "Hi."

I laughed at that and turned around. "Baby, take me to Miss Jackie's spot so I can get fresh; get some clean clothes.

Then I want us to roll out to the hospital so I can see my mother. I don't care what them doctors talking about. I gotta see her tonight."

* * *

I waited in the stairwell with sweat sliding down the side of my face. Took a deep breath and made Sodi get behind me. Opened the door to the stairwell and peeked down the long hallway. Seeing that it was empty, I waved Sodi to follow me. We crept down the long white hallway. Tip toeing, until we got to my mother's room. Once there I twisted the door handle and eased it open, allowing Sodi to slip inside, with me close behind her, after I looked both ways to make sure that the coast was clear. My mother was just on her way back from the bathroom when the both of us stepped inside of her room.

She stopped short. Bucked her swollen eyes as best she could. "Thylonius, is that you?" Her head was slightly bigger than Jelissa's had been. Both of her lips were swollen, and her eyes were black.

She looked so bad that I couldn't help but to break into tears. "Yeah, mama, it's me." I made my way across the room and took her into my arms.

She winced in pain, stepped back and held up her broken arm for me to see.

I lowered my head and kissed her cast. Made sure that I didn't bend her arm again accidentally and pulled her back into my embrace. "Mama, I'ma kill him this time. I swear to God, I'ma kill him. I'm tired of seeing you in this position." I broke down, holding her close to me. She felt as if she had lost twenty pounds. She was very skinny and brittle.

"That ain't gon' solve nothing, baby. I'm already on my way out and he ain't gon' be able to hurt your mother no more. It's my time." She hugged me as best she could, then eased out of my embrace and limped to her bed again.

Sodi rushed over to help her, then kissed both of her cheeks. I didn't know that they had become so familiar.

I kneeled in front of my mother and took her hand into mine. Kissed the back of it. "Mama, I love you so much. I don't like to hear you talking about leaving this earth. I don't know what I would do without you. You are my life."

"You're going to keep living, baby. You have to save your sister. You have to get yourself and her out of Chicago. It's not safe here for either of you. I would tell you to save your brothers too, but they are too far gone. They're evil. The devil has taken the better parts of them now." She broke into a fit of coughs

Sodi pat her back, then ran and got her some water. Helping her sip some of it.

"Mama, why did he do this to you this time?" I was struggling to look up at her. Nobody should have had to see their mother in such a physical state. I was crying more than I ever had in my entire life. The tears just wouldn't stop coming out of my eyes. I was angry. Deathly angry. How could any man do to a woman what my father had done to my mother, or what my brother had done to his baby mother? It was sick. In my opinion both of them niggas deserved death. They deserved to meet the Reaper, and I was the Reaper. I knew I had been real timid about killing them before, but now I wasn't. Now I looked forward to shedding blood from my own bloodline. They needed to be exterminated. They'd corrupted my fourteen-year-old sister and beaten my mother so bad that she was praying for death.

My mother shrugged. "Yo' daddy ain't never needed no reason to beat me before. He just came here, drunk, said that I ain't been home in too long, then beat me, and ran out of the hospital. I guess it was just time for me to get my butt kicked, son. I was long overdue." She looked off into space. "I'm ready to die, son. The cancer done spread all over my body. I can't eat. I can barely talk, and my chest hurt all the time. I'm ready to see Jesus. I done made my peace with this world." She broke into another fit of coughs again, hunched over.

Sodi held a napkin in front of her mouth. When she pulled it away it was spattered with blood. That broke me.

There was a knock on the door, and then a nurse stuck her head in. "Hey, what are you guys doing here? It's after visiting hours. You can't be here right now." The plump woman declared.

My mother held up a hand. "They're just leaving." She pulled me up as best she could. I stood before her. "Son, you have always been my protector. I love you. You need to let me go and save your sister. She needs you. Our Father in heaven is calling me home. I'm ready to go be with Him." She wrapped her arms around me and placed her lips to my ear. "Save her, baby. Only you can save her. I love you so much."

Chapter 16

I spent that whole night breaking down inside Miss Jackie's bathroom. We got the call that my mother had passed on two hours after we'd left her hospital room. A part of me felt like that she'd held on for as long as she did because she was waiting to see me for the last time. At least that thought gave my heart just a tad bit of peace. My mother was my everything. My heart and soul. There was nothing that I would not have done for her. Her whole life, all she'd known was pain and torment. Cursed, and born to parents that never loved, nor cared about her. Then cursed again to fall into love with a man that would be ten times worse than them. She'd been poor her entire life and had never seen outside of the slums of Chicago. As I knelt over the toilet, purging my guts, all of these thoughts played through my mind, torturing me.

Sodi knocked on the door about an hour after I'd finished throwing up. "Papi, let me in. I need to be in there comforting you. You matter to me. Please let me be there." She begged.

By this time, I was so sick and weak, that I needed somebody to hug on to. Somebody that cared about me. Somebody that understood what I was feeling in that moment. I needed to be loved. I was at my lowest point and falling fast. So, I opened the door.

She came in and fell to her knees, wrapping her arms around me. "I'm so sorry. Papi. I know you must be dying inside, but just know that I am here and that I ain't going nowhere. I love you with all of me. I mean that." She laid her head on my big chest. Started crying herself. For me this was big. I didn't understand how a female could feel for me the way that she appeared to be feeling for me. I didn't know what to think or what to do, so I just continued to break down with her in my arms until I couldn't cry no more.

Jelissa came to the bathroom door and knocked on it. "TJ, I got your sister on the phone. She's begging to talk to you."

I was so weak that I didn't even feel like talking to her. "Tell her I'll call her back in a few minutes. My head too fucked up right now." I felt sick again, like I needed to puke.

Sodi eased back and looked me over. "Baby, are you kidding? That's your sister. Your mother just told you to protect her. Get your ass up and go and get that phone. Now." She hopped up and pulled me along with her.

I lowered my head. "I can't think straight, Sodi. I gotta go identify my mother's body. Man, she was only thirty-four years old. This shit ain't fair." More tears dropped from my eyes. My knees got weak.

Sodi took a deep breath and held my face in both of her hands. She had a habit of doing this. "Papi, listen to me. It sucks that Deborah is gone. It really does. We're going to go and identify her body together. We're going to give her a funeral together. And we're going to bury her together. But, baby, the bottom line is that she's gone. She's no longer here. Marie is. Your mother told you specifically to save her. That was her dying wish. You have to do this for her."

More knocking on the door. "She says she really needs to talk to you, TJ. That it's a matter of life and death."

Sodi looked into my eyes. "Save that girl, TJ. You have to do this for your mother." She opened the door and handed me the phone. "Here, Papi, I'm here with you."

Man, I was glad that she was because my brain was all screwed up in the worst way. I needed her guidance. She was like an angel sent from heaven. I was falling for her hard. I took the phone and placed it to my ear. "You know our mother is dead, don't you?" A lone tear slid down my cheek. Sodi wiped it away

Marie was quiet for a brief second. "No, I didn't know that. When did she pass?" Her voice was scratchy. Almost as if it were filled with sleep.

"A few hours ago. I'm about to go down there and identify the body. You should come, too. I miss you, lil' sis."

She was real quiet. But then I could hear her sniffling away from the phone. She appeared to be crying. "I'm pregnant, TJ, and Deion says that he's going to kick this baby out of me. Daddy knows about it, and he says that the next time he sees me, he's going to shoot me down where I stand. I'm so scared that I don't know what to do. I feel trapped. You have to come and get me before something serious happens. I don't know what to do and I'm freaking out big time. I think when he gets back that he's going to do something to me."

I perked up and got angry quick. "Who? Who finna do something to you?" My heart was pounding in my chest.

"Deion. I think he's going to kill me, TJ, and I'm not kidding. I heard Daddy telling him that he needed to get rid of me. I don't know what that means, but I can only imagine. You know how our family gets down. Especially them. Deion doesn't want it to get out that he may have me pregnant. And Daddy is jealous, and crazy. He's been wanting to do something to me for a long time, but Deion hasn't let him. Now I think they both are going to kill me and get rid of my body like they did Kia's."

I didn't know who Kia was, but it was blowing my mind that this conversation was actually happening. How the fuck could all of the men in my family be corrupting my little sister like this to the point that they were about to kill her out of jealousy of one another, and stupidity? I was thrown. "Sis, where are you right now?"

"I'm at Deion's place in Riverdale. He took all of my clothes and shoes and locked me in this room from the outside. The windows have bars on them, and outside of the bars are boards. I can't even tell if it's night or day. The only way I was able to call you is because when he let me out to use the bathroom, he was on the phone in the kitchen and I smuggled my phone back into the room before he locked the door again. What do I do? Should I call the cops?" She whimpered.

I was so lost and mad that I couldn't think straight. I was seeing red. My heart was banging against my ribcage. "N'all, fuck the law, I'ma be over there as soon as I get done identifying mama's body. I should be your way in like two hours. Do you think you can hold up until then?"

There was a loud slam in her background. She yelped. "Who is there?" She hollered.

I couldn't hear their response. "Who did they say, lil' sis?" I made my way into the guest room, getting dressed with one hand.

"Baby what's the matter? Is she okay?" Sodi asked, rubbing my back.

I held up a finger to silence her. She nodded in understanding and sat on the bed beside Jelissa who was rocking her son to sleep. "Marie, who is it?" I was getting worried.

"JD and Daddy. They unlocking the locks on this bedroom. I think they finna do something to me, TJ. Please get here soon." She cried. "Y'all leave me alone until Deion get back."

I heard a bunch of commotion in the background.

"Come here, bitch! It's my turn now. Then Pops'. Then we gon' dump yo' ass in the river. Ma'fuckas done with you!" JD hollered, and Marie screamed.

"Bitch ass nigga, leave my sister alone!" I snapped.

This made Rae'Jon wake up crying at the top of his lungs. Jelissa scooped him and ran out of the room, apologizing.

I grabbed a .40 Glock out of the top dresser drawer and slid it into the small of my back. "Yo, I gotta go get my sister. She think my brother and father about to do something serious to her. And she pregnant right now. Everything is fucked up."

Sodi's eyes got as big as saucers. "Baby, I'm sorry. Is there anything I can do to help you?" She asked, throwing her spring jacket on.

"Just stay here and make sure that Jelissa and her son are okay. I'ma send Juelz a quick text and have him meet me in the Hunnits. Baby, I'm finna get rid of these niggas once and for all. Then I'ma go and identify my mother's body."

Sodi blocked my way as I was headed out of the bedroom. "Papi, wait. Can I please go with you? I feel like something major is about to happen, and I just want to be by your side. Please don't deny me of this." Her voice was shaky. I could tell that she was on the verge of breaking down. She was very emotional, and honestly it was one of the things that I loved about her. I needed that because at times I was so heartless that I needed to be balanced out. She kept me grounded.

"Baby, I need you to be here where you are safe and sound. I don't know what is about to transpire. But whatever it is, I'm gon' survive it, and when I do, I need to know that you're going to be waiting for me on the other end. You hear me?" I snatched her up and kissed her juicy lips. Seeking strength from them and got some. I honestly was starting to see just how much she was needed in my life.

She hugged me tight. "Baby, please be safe. Please don't lose this war, or whatever it is. I need you. You're my Papi now.

I kissed her forehead. "I won't, baby. But I gotta do what I gotta do. Just pray for me."

* * *

Juelz pulled behind Miss Jackie's truck a half hour later. Jumped out of his whip with a long black trench coat on and knocked on the passenger's window hard. I popped the lock, and he climbed in and showed me the assault rifle that he'd had hidden in his coat. "Bruh, I'm telling you now that I'm shooting to kill. I hate your brothers. Them niggas real foul, and now that I know what they been doing to Marie, all I can think about is murder. When we get over her, I'm looking to kill, TJ. Fuck everything else. No nuts, no glory. That's my word. I'ma ask you one time, are you all in like a Poker hand?"

I nodded. "Hell yeah. But we gotta hold fast until we get Marie out of their care. As soon as she's out of danger, then we can let these bullets fly. Fuck them niggas. On everything." I pulled away from the curb and through the streetlights. It was four in the morning and beginning to rain. "How many shots that bitch hold?" I asked looking to him.

"Fifty. But I got two magazines in my pocket. I wanna make these niggas my Covergirls. Word up."

I snickered at that and frowned. "My moms passed away a few hours ago. She said she couldn't take it no more and gave up her fight to Jehovah. I'm fucked up, bruh. I feel like I'm losing my mind." The rain began to come down a bit harder. I flipped on the windshield wipers and added some heat.

"Yo, I'm sorry to hear that, bruh. She was a good woman. A queen. It sucks that she had your old man as a husband. Anybody could see that he didn't deserve her."

"I know. He beat her senseless while she was on her death bed. What type of nigga a get down like that on the mother of his children? I should've smoked that fool when I had the chance before he took the stand on me. Something told me to smoke him, too. Had I did it, my mother would still be alive." I shook my head. "What you got to smoke on?"

He took a fat ass Garcia Vega from his inside trench coat pocket. "Here, this that Brooklyn right here." He flicked his lighter and held it to the tip of the blunt while I puffed on it. "This shit gon' fuck you up, so take it easy. I don't want you being off of your square and shooting innocent bystanders and shit. A few pulls should be good for you."

I slowed the truck so I could stop at the red lights. Once I stopped, I let him hold the flame to the end, and I started to toke on it to get the cigar lit. Smoke wafted toward the roof of the truck. The weed smelled stanky and started cutting into my throat right away. I closed my eyes and started to cough. I heard the screeching of brakes. That made me open my eyes back up.

Juelz jumped closer to the passenger's door and struggled to get the big assault rifle up. "Aw, shit! It's a hit, TJ! It's a hit!"

The next thing I knew, there was a bunch of gunfire, and the windows shattered inside the truck. Hot liquid sprayed across my face, and I felt the burning sensation of lead entering into my body back to back.

To be continued …
Born Heartless 2
Coming Soon

Submission Guideline

Submit the first three chapters of your completed manuscript to ldpsubmissions@gmail.com, subject line: Your book's title. The manuscript must be in a .doc file and sent as an attachment. Document should be in Times New Roman, double spaced and in size 12 font. Also, provide your synopsis and full contact information. If sending multiple submissions, they must each be in a separate email.

Have a story but no way to send it electronically? You can still submit to LDP/Ca$h Presents. Send in the first three chapters, written or typed, of your completed manuscript to:

LDP: Submissions Dept
Po Box 870494
Mesquite, Tx 75187

DO NOT send original manuscript. Must be a duplicate.

Provide your synopsis and a cover letter containing your full contact information.

Thanks for considering LDP and Ca$h Presents.

Coming Soon from Lock Down Publications/Ca$h Presents

BOW DOWN TO MY GANGSTA

By **Ca$h**

TORN BETWEEN TWO

By **Coffee**

BLOOD STAINS OF A SHOTTA **III**

By **Jamaica**

STEADY MOBBIN **III**

By **Marcellus Allen**

RENEGADE BOYS IV

By Meesha

BLOOD OF A BOSS **VI**

SHADOWS OF THE GAME II

By **Askari**

LOYAL TO THE GAME **IV**

LIFE OF SIN **III**

By **T.J. & Jelissa**

A DOPEBOY'S PRAYER **II**

By **Eddie "Wolf" Lee**

IF LOVING YOU IS WRONG… **III**

By **Jelissa**

TRUE SAVAGE **VII**

By **Chris Green**

BLAST FOR ME **III**

DUFFLE BAG CARTEL **IV**

HEARTLESS GOON **II**

By **Ghost**

A HUSTLER'S DECEIT III

KILL ZONE **II**

BAE BELONGS TO ME III

SOUL OF A MONSTER III

By **Aryanna**

THE COST OF LOYALTY **III**

By **Kweli**

A GANGSTER'S SYN III

By **J-Blunt**

KING OF NEW YORK V

RISE TO POWER III

COKE KINGS III

BORN HEARTLESS II

By **T.J. Edwards**

GORILLAZ IN THE BAY IV

De'Kari

THE STREETS ARE CALLING II

Duquie Wilson

KINGPIN KILLAZ IV

STREET KINGS III

PAID IN BLOOD II

Hood Rich

SINS OF A HUSTLA II

ASAD

TRIGGADALE III

Elijah R. Freeman

MARRIED TO A BOSS III

By Destiny Skai & Chris Green

KINGZ OF THE GAME IV

Playa Ray

SLAUGHTER GANG III

RUTHLESS HEART

By Willie Slaughter

THE HEART OF A SAVAGE II

By Jibril Williams

FUK SHYT II

By Blakk Diamond

THE DOPEMAN'S BODYGAURD II

By Tranay Adams

TRAP GOD

By Troublesome

YAYO

By S. Allen

GHOST MOB

Stilloan Robinson

KINGPIN DREAMS

By Paper Boi Rari

CREAM

By Yolanda Moore

Available Now

RESTRAINING ORDER **I & II**

By **CA$H & Coffee**

LOVE KNOWS NO BOUNDARIES **I II & III**

By **Coffee**

RAISED AS A GOON I, II, III & IV

BRED BY THE SLUMS I, II, III

BLAST FOR ME I & II

ROTTEN TO THE CORE I II III

A BRONX TALE I, II, III

DUFFEL BAG CARTEL I II III

HEARTLESS GOON

A SAVAGE DOPEBOY

HEARTLESS GOON

By **Ghost**

LAY IT DOWN **I & II**

LAST OF A DYING BREED

BLOOD STAINS OF A SHOTTA I & II

By **Jamaica**

LOYAL TO THE GAME

LOYAL TO THE GAME II

LOYAL TO THE GAME III

LIFE OF SIN I, II

By **TJ & Jelissa**

BLOODY COMMAS I & II

SKI MASK CARTEL I II & III

KING OF NEW YORK I II,III IV

RISE TO POWER I II

COKE KINGS I II

BORN HEARTLESS

By **T.J. Edwards**

IF LOVING HIM IS WRONG…I & II

LOVE ME EVEN WHEN IT HURTS I II III

By **Jelissa**

WHEN THE STREETS CLAP BACK I & II III

By **Jibril Williams**

A DISTINGUISHED THUG STOLE MY HEART I II & III

LOVE SHOULDN'T HURT I II III IV

RENEGADE BOYS I II III

By **Meesha**

A GANGSTER'S CODE I &, II III

A GANGSTER'S SYN II

By J-Blunt

PUSH IT TO THE LIMIT

By **Bre' Hayes**

BLOOD OF A BOSS **I, II, III, IV, V**

SHADOWS OF THE GAME

By **Askari**

THE STREETS BLEED MURDER **I, II & III**

THE HEART OF A GANGSTA I II& III

By **Jerry Jackson**

CUM FOR ME

CUM FOR ME 2

CUM FOR ME 3

CUM FOR ME 4

CUM FOR ME 5

An **LDP Erotica Collaboration**

BRIDE OF A HUSTLA **I II & II**

THE FETTI GIRLS **I, II& III**

CORRUPTED BY A GANGSTA I, II III, IV

BLINDED BY HIS LOVE

By **Destiny Skai**

WHEN A GOOD GIRL GOES BAD

By **Adrienne**

THE COST OF LOYALTY I II
By Kweli
A GANGSTER'S REVENGE **I II III & IV**
THE BOSS MAN'S DAUGHTERS
THE BOSS MAN'S DAUGHTERS II
THE BOSSMAN'S DAUGHTERS III
THE BOSSMAN'S DAUGHTERS IV
THE BOSS MAN'S DAUGHTERS **V**
A SAVAGE LOVE **I & II**
BAE BELONGS TO ME I II
A HUSTLER'S DECEIT I, II, III
WHAT BAD BITCHES DO I, II, III
SOUL OF A MONSTER I II
KILL ZONE
By **Aryanna**
A KINGPIN'S AMBITON
A KINGPIN'S AMBITION **II**
I MURDER FOR THE DOUGH
By **Ambitious**
TRUE SAVAGE
TRUE SAVAGE II
TRUE SAVAGE **III**
TRUE SAVAGE **IV**
TRUE SAVAGE **V**
TRUE SAVAGE **VI**
By **Chris Green**
A DOPEBOY'S PRAYER
By **Eddie "Wolf" Lee**
THE KING CARTEL **I, II & III**

Born Heartless

By **Frank Gresham**

THESE NIGGAS AIN'T LOYAL **I, II & III**

By **Nikki Tee**

GANGSTA SHYT **I II &III**

By **CATO**

THE ULTIMATE BETRAYAL

By **Phoenix**

BOSS'N UP **I , II & III**

By **Royal Nicole**

I LOVE YOU TO DEATH

By Destiny J

I RIDE FOR MY HITTA

I STILL RIDE FOR MY HITTA

By **Misty Holt**

LOVE & CHASIN' PAPER

By **Qay Crockett**

TO DIE IN VAIN

SINS OF A HUSTLA

By **ASAD**

BROOKLYN HUSTLAZ

By **Boogsy Morina**

BROOKLYN ON LOCK I & II

By **Sonovia**

GANGSTA CITY

By **Teddy Duke**

A DRUG KING AND HIS DIAMOND I & II III

A DOPEMAN'S RICHES

HER MAN, MINE'S TOO I, II

CASH MONEY HO'S

By Nicole Goosby

TRAPHOUSE KING **I II & III**

KINGPIN KILLAZ I II III

STREET KINGS I II

PAID IN BLOOD

By **Hood Rich**

LIPSTICK KILLAH **I, II, III**

CRIME OF PASSION I & II

By **Mimi**

STEADY MOBBN' **I, II, III**

By **Marcellus Allen**

WHO SHOT YA **I, II, III**

Renta

GORILLAZ IN THE BAY **I II III**

DE'KARI

TRIGGADALE I II

Elijah R. Freeman

GOD BLESS THE TRAPPERS I, II, III

THESE SCANDALOUS STREETS I, II, III

FEAR MY GANGSTA I, II, III

THESE STREETS DON'T LOVE NOBODY I, II

BURY ME A G I, II, III, IV, V

A GANGSTA'S EMPIRE I, II, III, IV

THE DOPEMAN'S BODYGAURD

Tranay Adams

THE STREETS ARE CALLING

Duquie Wilson

MARRIED TO A BOSS… I II

By Destiny Skai & Chris Green

KINGZ OF THE GAME I II III

Playa Ray

SLAUGHTER GANG I II

By Willie Slaughter

THE HEART OF A SAVAGE

By Jibril Williams

FUK SHYT

By Blakk Diamond

DON'T F#CK WITH MY HEART I II

By Linnea

ADDICTED TO THE DRAMA I II III

By Jamila

<u>BOOKS BY LDP'S CEO, CA$H</u>

<u>TRUST IN NO MAN</u>

<u>TRUST IN NO MAN 2</u>

<u>TRUST IN NO MAN 3</u>

<u>BONDED BY BLOOD</u>

<u>SHORTY GOT A THUG</u>

<u>THUGS CRY</u>

<u>THUGS CRY 2</u>

<u>THUGS CRY 3</u>

<u>TRUST NO BITCH</u>

<u>TRUST NO BITCH 2</u>

<u>TRUST NO BITCH 3</u>

<u>TIL MY CASKET DROPS</u>

<u>RESTRAINING ORDER</u>

<u>RESTRAINING ORDER 2</u>

<u>IN LOVE WITH A CONVICT</u>

<u>Coming Soon</u>

BONDED BY BLOOD 2

BOW DOWN TO MY GANGSTA

CPSIA information can be obtained
at www.ICGtesting.com
Printed in the USA
LVHW010851160521
687568LV00010B/871